ROMA[obscured]
NEW Y[obscured]

"Smith fulfills [obscured]
this fast-paced [obscured]

LAWLESS, TEXAS

"Readers will be entertained and find themselves cheering for the good guys in the final shootout."

HIRED GUN

"Nobody does a Western better than Smith."

DEFIANT

"The talented Smith is in her element out West. This novel is fast-paced and filled with adventure and tender feelings . . . a very beautiful story."

HALFBREED WARRIOR

"Smith is the consummate storyteller. The pacing is quick, with snappy dialogue moving the story forward at breakneck speed."

BRAZEN

"As sexy and gritty as [Smith] has ever written."

HALF-MOON RANCH: HUNTER'S MOON

"Bobbi Smith is a terrific storyteller whose wonderful characters, good dialogue and compelling plot will keep you up all night."

FOREVER AUTUMN

"*Forever Autumn* is a fast-paced, delightful story."

LONE WARRIOR

"Fast paced, swift moving and filled with strong, well-crafted characters."

EDEN

"The very talented Bobbi Smith has written another winner. *Eden* is filled with adventure, danger, sentimentality and romance."

THE HALF-BREED

"Witty, tender, strong characters and plenty of action, as well as superb storytelling, make this a keeper."

BRIDES OF DURANGO: JENNY

"Bobbi Smith has another winner. This third installment is warm and tender as only Ms. Smith can do. . . . Fans will not be disappointed."

BRIDES OF DURANGO: TESSA

"Another wonderful read by consummate storyteller Bobbi Smith. . . . Filled with adventure and romance, more than one couple winds up happily-ever-after in this gem."

BRIDES OF DURANGO: ELISE

"There's plenty of action, danger and heated romance as the pages fly by. This is exactly what fans expect from Bobbi Smith."

WESTON'S LADY

"Bobbi Smith has penned another winner."

HALF-BREED'S LADY

"A fast-paced, frying-pan-into-the-fire adventure that runs the gamut of emotions, from laughter to tears. A must-read for Ms. Smith's fans, and a definite keeper."

OUTLAW'S LADY

"Bobbi Smith is an author of many talents; one of them being able to weave more than one story. . . . Ms. Smith creates characters that one will remember for some time to come."

THE LADY & THE TEXAN

"An action-packed read with roller-coaster adventures that keep you turning the pages. *The Lady & the Texan* is just plain enjoyable."

RENEGADE'S LADY

"A wonderfully delicious 'Perils of Pauline' style romance. With dashes of humor, passion, adventure and romance, Ms. Smith creates another winner that only she could write!"

A mail-order bride?

What in the world would an outlaw want with a wife?

Lane didn't know how he did it, but he managed to keep the smile on his face as he dealt with the news. He stayed in control and calmly turned to the young woman who was sitting with Gertrude in the buggy.

"Miss Lawrence," he greeted the slightly nervous-looking blonde. "It's nice to finally meet you."

Destiny had watched the two cowboys come out of the stable as they'd driven up. She hadn't known if one of them was the man who, within a matter of hours, would be her husband, but she did now, and she was shocked.

Ever since they'd left St. Louis, she'd tried to imagine what a man who had to order a wife would look like. The image she'd come up with had, at times, been more than a little scary. She'd fully expected Seth Rawlins to be a desperate man, but as she gazed at the good-looking rancher standing before her, she knew she'd been wrong. There was nothing desperate about Seth Rawlins. He was tall and powerfully built and ruggedly handsome.

Other books by Bobbi Smith:

RAPTURE'S TEMPEST
WANTED: THE HALF-BREED
LAWLESS, TEXAS
HIRED GUN
DEFIANT
HALFBREED WARRIOR
BRAZEN
BAYOU BRIDE
HUNTER'S MOON (HALF MOON RANCH)
FOREVER AUTUMN
LONE WARRIOR
EDEN
WANTON SPLENDOR
SWEET SILKEN BONDAGE
THE HALF-BREED (SECRET FIRES)
WESTON'S LADY
HALF-BREED'S LADY
OUTLAW'S LADY
FORBIDDEN FIRES
RAPTURE'S RAGE
THE LADY & THE TEXAN
RENEGADE'S LADY
THE LADY'S HAND
LADY DECEPTION

The Brides of Durango series:

ELISE
TESSA
JENNY

Writing as Julie Marshall:

MIRACLES
HAVEN

BOBBI SMITH

RUNAWAY

LEISURE BOOKS NEW YORK CITY

A LEISURE BOOK®

July 2009

Published by

Dorchester Publishing Co., Inc.
200 Madison Avenue
New York, NY 10016

ISBN 10: 0-8439-6281-X
ISBN 13: 978-0-8439-6281-9
E-ISBN: 978-1-4285-0695-4

Printed in the United States of America.

10 9 8 7 6 5 4 3 2 1

This book is dedicated to my cousin Charlotte Savage. Love ya! And to everyone at St. Joseph's—especially the Sunday morning gang, the Wednesday morning gang, everybody at PSR, CHRP and the Prayer Chain. You're wonderful! Thanks!

Also, thanks to all the wonderful librarians in the St. Charles County Library District and the St. Louis Public Libraries who helped me with my research, especially Judy Brown, Cindy Menkhus, Larry Franke and Ann Randolph.

Author's Note

I recently discovered Country/Western singer Royal Wade Kimes. If you like songs about the Wild West check him out. His CD *How The West Was Sung* is great!

RUNAWAY

Prologue

Texas, Early 1870s

Lane Madison and two of his ranch hands urged their horses to a quicker pace as they covered the final miles to the Bar M ranch house. They'd been gone for three days, working stock, and were looking forward to finally getting back home.

"It's going to be real nice, having a home-cooked meal tonight," Lane said, knowing it was almost suppertime and Katie would be hard at work, cooking.

"You sure made a smart decision when you married Katie," Rick Meyers told him. "She's not only pretty, she can cook, too."

Lane was smiling as he thought of his beautiful dark-haired wife. He looked over at Rick and warned good-naturedly, "You don't have your sights set on my wife, do you?"

"I'd love to set my sights on Katie, but I know how

good she can handle a cast-iron skillet, and I'm not going anywhere near her unless I'm invited."

They all laughed, remembering how deftly Katie had subdued one of the rowdier ranch hands who'd gotten drunk and had made the mistake of trying to cause some trouble on the ranch a few weeks ago when Lane had been away.

"I bet Mose had a headache for quite a few days after she hit him," Lane said.

"You know he did, and I'm real glad we ain't seen him since," Rick agreed.

"Yep, you got yourself one fine filly in Katie," added Buck Wilson, the other hand. "Maybe one of these days, me and Rick will get lucky and find ourselves good women like her, too."

Lane grew even more eager to see Katie as they rode on. They'd been married just over a year, and she was now pregnant with their first child. Knowing he would soon be a father drove him to work even harder at making the Bar M a success. He wanted the ranch to be a safe haven for his family.

As they topped a low rise, they spotted the ranch house and outbuildings in the distance.

"Looks like we're home, boys," Lane said as they rode in.

But when they drew closer, Lane thought it was odd that there weren't many of the hands around. He grew even more concerned when Andy, the stable hand, came hurrying out of the stable to meet them as they reined in.

"Mark and the boys didn't find you?" Andy asked worriedly.

"No, we didn't see anyone else on the ride in. Why?" Lane answered. "Was there trouble while we were gone?" He could tell Andy was nervous about something.

"Yeah, you'd better get up to the house—"

"Katie—Is Katie all right?"

"Helen's up there with Doc Halsey—" Andy warned him.

Lane didn't wait to hear any more. If the doctor was there along with his foreman's wife, something was wrong—badly wrong. He ran toward the house.

Helen Carter, the foreman's wife, had been up at the house helping Doc Halsey. When she saw Lane and the other men ride in, she hurried upstairs to let the doctor know.

"Lane's back—" she whispered from the bedroom doorway. She was the one who'd found Katie early that morning, battered, raped and left for dead, all alone in the main house. She'd sent for the doctor immediately and had been doing all she could to help Katie ever since.

The doctor looked down at the bed where Katie lay so pale and deathly still, and then he got up.

"Stay with her—just in case . . ." He left the room to speak with Lane.

Doc Halsey had just come down the steps and reached the front hall when Lane rushed into the house.

"Doc—What is it? What happened?" Lane demanded, looking past him up the stairs for some sign of his wife.

"We need to talk, Lane," the older man said quietly, directing him toward the parlor.

Lane resisted. "But I want to see Katie. Where is she?"

"Let's go in the parlor for a minute."

Lane looked up the stairs again and then took his hat off and left it on the hallway table before reluctantly following the doctor's order. He was tense and on edge, fearing the news the man was about to give him. He worried Katie had fallen or possibly had a miscarriage.

"Sit down," the doc directed. He thought it would be best if Lane was sitting down when he told him the news.

But Lane refused. "No. I'll stand. Tell me what happened. What's wrong?"

Doc Halsey knew there was no easy way to tell Lane what had happened. "Katie's been injured—She's in very serious condition right now."

"Injured? What are you talking about? How was she hurt?"

"Evidently, from what we've been able to figure out, last night one of the ranch hands you fired, a man named Mose Harper, came back." The doc went on to tell Lane how the man had abused and beaten Katie and how she'd lost the baby.

Fury filled Lane, and he felt sick inside. The fact that he and the boys had just been talking about Mose, and had been laughing about what had happened, made him feel even worse. "Oh, my God—"

"Helen found Katie this morning, and from what little Katie was able to tell her, Mose sneaked into the house sometime after dark. He cornered her in the parlor, and she didn't have the chance to scream, caught off guard the way she was. She put up a fight, but . . ."

"I've got to see her . . ." He turned to go.

"Lane—"

The tone of the doctor's voice stopped him cold, and Lane turned to look back at him.

"She may not make it through the day."

This was the news he'd been dreading.

Lane said nothing more.

He couldn't.

He turned his back on the doctor and went upstairs. Inwardly, he was shaking as he came to stand in the bedroom doorway.

The sight that greeted Lane devastated him. Helen was seated in a chair, keeping vigil at the bedside where Katie lay unmoving. Katie's eyes were closed, her coloring was ashen, and her face was bruised and battered from the abuse she'd suffered at Mose's hands.

Helen had heard Lane coming, and she quickly stood up and went to him. She touched him gently on the arm, wanting to comfort him in some way. "Thank God, you're back. She's been asking for you."

"She's conscious?" he managed.

"She's in and out—She's in a lot of pain—"

He nodded and walked past her to the bedside. He sat down in the chair there and took Katie's hand in his. Her hand was limp, and the knowledge that she was so weak tore at him.

"Katie—" He spoke her name in a strangled whisper, but there was no response. "Katie—I'm here—"

Katie's breathing was so shallow, Lane could hardly hear it. The horror of what Mose had done to her ravaged him. He had thought she was safe here on the ranch. He'd never believed the drunken ranch hand would come back again, let alone try to harm her.

Guilt assailed Lane as he sat by his wife's side. He could only imagine what she'd suffered at Mose's hands, and he knew somehow, someway, he was going to find the drunk and make him pay for what he'd done.

He remained there, holding her cold, limp hand in his, waiting and praying for a miracle.

Helen found the doctor sitting in the parlor. "What should we do?"

"There's nothing we can do but wait," Doc Halsey said sadly. "It's in God's hands now."

Helen glanced back up the steps, her heart breaking, her eyes filled with tears. "I know."

Katie stirred and opened her eyes to see Lane in the chair beside her. Summoning what little strength she had left, she whispered his name, "Lane . . ."

He had been sitting there quietly, waiting, her hand in his, when the sound of her voice sent a surge of joy and hope through him. He shifted closer. "Katie—"

"You're here . . ." She gazed up at the man she loved, knowing her time was near.

"I'm here, love. I'm here, and I'll never leave you alone again," he promised. "I'm sorry . . ."

Katie realized he was blaming himself. "Not your fault—Mose—It was Mose—"

He looked down at her, guilt and pain filling him. He knew now that he should never have left her, that he should have been there to protect her and keep her and their unborn child safe.

"I love you, Lane . . ." she told him, and those

words were her last. A moment later, she closed her eyes, and her life slipped away.

"I love you, too . . ." Lane began.

Then as he stared down at her, he realized she'd drawn her last breath.

"Katie . . ."

Agony tore through him. He took her up in his arms, and he clutched her to him. He called out for the doctor as he held her to his heart.

Doc Halsey heard Lane's urgent call and knew what had happened. He had feared Katie wouldn't be able to hold on much longer, since she'd lost so much blood. He rushed up the stairs now to see if there was anything he could do.

The sight that greeted him was heartbreaking. Lane was there at the bedside, holding Katie's limp form in his arms. He hurried to Lane's side and took her from him to lay her back upon the bed. Doc Halsey was clinging to the slim hope that somehow she might still survive, that she would have enough strength to keep fighting, but as he gazed down at her, he knew she was gone.

The doctor looked up at Lane, and their gazes met. "I'm sorry—"

The finality of Katie's death struck Lane almost physically. He collapsed into the chair, burying his head in his hands as he gave in to his sorrow.

Doc Halsey backed out of the room and closed the

door behind him as he moved into the hall, leaving Lane alone to grieve.

Two Days Later

Lane came out of the house, carrying his saddlebags and rifle. He was going after Mose, and he wouldn't be back until he'd found the man who'd killed Katie. He went straight to the stable where his men had gathered, their mood quiet and somber.

Rick was there, waiting for him. He had their horses saddled, and he, too, was ready to ride.

Lane looked at him, his gaze cold. "You think you're going with me?"

"I know I am," Rick answered. He was determined not to let his friend ride out alone.

On the day Helen had found Katie, two of the hands had immediately set out after Mose to try to track him down and bring him back, while another hand had gone into town to let the sheriff know what had happened. Lane hadn't learned of this until after Katie's passing, but once he had, he'd been glad they'd gone after Mose while his trail was still fresh. He'd been glad, too, when the sheriff immediately put up a wanted poster on the man.

Lane had hoped the ranch hands who'd ridden after Mose would find him quickly and bring him back to face justice, but it hadn't happened. The two men who'd been tracking him had lost his trail after a storm had swept through, and they'd been unable to find it again.

Once they'd returned to the Bar M and told Lane what had happened, he'd known what he had to do.

He was going after Mose himself.

He would not rest until he'd found the man responsible for the deaths of Katie and his unborn child.

"With the wanted poster up, the law will be looking for him," Mark told him seriously. "You don't have to do this."

"Yes. I do," was Lane's terse answer. He turned a cold-eyed glare on his friend. "Take care of things here while I'm gone."

Mark knew then there was nothing more he could say or do to stop Lane from leaving.

Katie's death had changed Lane.

The ranch meant nothing to him now.

All he cared about was finding the man responsible for his wife's death.

"I will," Mark promised.

Lane and Mark were both grim as they shook hands. Then Mark stepped back to watch as Lane and Rick mounted up and rode out.

Six Weeks Later

The long days in the saddle covering endless miles in their pursuit of Mose had left Lane and Rick trail weary, but Lane was not about to let up. He had a gut feeling that they were closing in on Katie's killer, and he was determined to keep going.

"This may be it," he told Rick as they neared the outskirts of the town of Sagebrush.

"How do you want to do this?"

"Let's start at the saloon. Knowing Mose, that'd be the first place he'd go."

Lane knew better than to get his hopes up too high, but when he spotted Mose's horse tied out in front of the saloon, he knew the murderer's days of running were over.

"Look," he told Rick, pointing out the horse.

"You were right. We've got him now."

They dismounted out front, and Lane led the way inside.

Mose was feeling real good about himself as he sat in the saloon in Sagebrush. After all this time, no one from the Bar M had come after him to try to take him in, so he figured he'd gotten away with paying the Madison gal back.

Mose took another deep drink of his whiskey as he eyed the buxom blonde saloon girl walking past his table. Unable to resist, he reached out and grabbed her, pulling her onto his lap. He pressed some wet, sloppy kisses down her neck and began to openly grope her.

"Behave yourself, big boy," Sally said, disgusted by his ways.

Her use of 'big boy' infuriated Mose. He wasn't a tall man, and he hated it when anyone taunted him about his height. Her protest just made him all the more determined to have his way with her. He liked being in control. He liked making women beg. It made him feel powerful, like he really was a big man.

"Why don't I go get you another drink?" she offered, hoping the excuse would get her away from him. She'd dealt with many disgusting men over the years, but having watched this one over the last few nights, she knew he was one of the worst.

Mose heard her request, but he had no intention of letting her go. He was enjoying himself too much. He tightened his grip on her and forced her to stay on his lap. "You ain't going anywhere, baby doll. You're going to stay right here with me until I'm ready to take you upstairs."

Inwardly, she groaned. She was miserable at the prospect of suffering a mauling at his hands. "But you need a refill—"

"No, I don't. I need you. Now!" He was drunked up enough to believe he could take her right there in the saloon with everybody watching. He tried to push her dress completely off her shoulders to bare her breasts.

"No! Stop it!" She started to resist him, shoving away his hands with all her strength.

"Don't you tell me 'no,' woman!" Mose snarled, and he got even rougher with her.

"You heard the lady, Mose."

A voice that was horribly familiar to him called out from the front of the saloon and sent a jolt of terror through Mose. He went still.

"Let her go . . . ," Lane ordered.

Mose let his hands drop away from the blonde.

Sally jumped up from his lap and fled to safety, staring wide-eyed in wonder at the tall, dark man who'd issued the order. She could tell the stranger meant business. He and another man were standing at the front of the saloon just inside the swinging doors with their guns drawn and aimed at the drunk.

Mose hadn't looked toward Lane yet, and now he smiled slowly to himself. He hadn't let the saloon girl go because Lane had ordered it. He had let her go so he could reach for his gun. "Well, well, well, if it ain't my old boss . . ."

His snide, arrogant ways only infuriated Lane more. "That's right. Now, turn around real slow and keep your hands where I can see them."

Mose slowly shifted positions and looked Lane's way. It was then that he saw Rick standing beside Lane in front of the bar. Both men had their guns trained on him.

"Who are you boys, and what are you doing in my saloon?" the bartender demanded.

"We've come for our friend here," Lane told him, nodding toward Mose.

"Are you the law?"

"No," Lane answered, "but here's the wanted poster."

Without looking away from Mose, Lane pulled the folded-up sheet of paper from his shirt pocket and tossed it on the bar in front of him.

The bartender snatched the poster up to read it.

"All right," the bartender said, after studying the likeness of Mose Harper on the poster and then looking over at the man sitting at the table in the back of the saloon. "You!" he ordered one of the men who was standing at the bar, drinking. "Go find the sheriff—and get him back here fast!"

The man at the bar ran out the swinging doors to do what the bartender had ordered.

Mose knew just how wrong he'd been to think Lane Madison wouldn't find him. He had thought he'd gotten away with teaching Lane's wife a lesson, but now as he faced his old boss, he was scared, real scared. He slowly got to his feet and turned around slowly.

"Lane—Rick, what's this all about?" Mose wanted to go for his gun, but he had to make his move when the time was right, or he'd be a dead man.

"Don't play innocent with me, Mose," Lane ground out. "Katie's dead."

"Dead?" he squeaked like the coward he was.

"That's right, and you're the one who killed her."

"I didn't kill her," Mose lied. He'd thought for sure she'd been dead when he'd left her, so he had no idea how Lane could have found out that he was the one who'd raped and beaten her. Even so, the look in Lane's eyes heightened the terror that filled him.

"Katie lived long enough to tell me what you did," Lane said, rage filling him. "And I'm going to see you pay for it. I'm going to enjoy watching you hang."

Mose knew right then he was a dead man—one way or the other. His only hope was to shoot his way out of this, so in a fierce, quick move, he went for his gun.

But Lane had expected Mose would try to run off, and he was ready for him. When Mose went for his gun, Lane fired, and he watched in satisfaction as the drunk collapsed on the floor, moaning.

Lane and Rick walked slowly to where Mose lay, their guns still in hand. Lane stood over him, while Rick made short order of grabbing up Mose's gun from where he'd dropped it when he'd been hit.

Mose looked up at Lane, quaking and trembling in terror as he clutched his bloody shoulder and cowered before him.

"Don't kill me! Don't kill me!" he squealed.

Lane stared down at the man who had so cold-bloodedly taken Katie's life.

He wanted him to pay for what he'd done.

He wanted him to suffer.

Lane's grip on his gun tightened.

He wanted to put an end to the drunk's miserable, worthless life, but he managed to control himself. "Don't worry, Mose. I'm not going to kill you."

Mose was stunned. He stared up at Lane wide-eyed.

"No, I'm not going to kill you," Lane repeated. "That would be too easy for you. I'm going to let the law deal with you. You're going to hang."

"Nooo!" the coward wailed, crying and shaking in his fear.

As he was squealing, the town's sheriff came rushing in. He'd heard the gunfire and had drawn his revolver, ready for trouble.

"What's going on?" he demanded, seeing the wounded man on the floor and the stranger standing over him, gun in hand.

"It's all right now, Sheriff," the bartender hurried to reassure him as he handed over the wanted poster. "Here—"

The sheriff quickly read the description of the wanted man and then looked down at Mose in disgust.

"Mose Harper—You're under arrest for murder. I'm taking you in." He glanced over at some of the other men in the bar and ordered, "You two, get him up and take him over to the jail. I'll be right there to lock him up."

The men quickly did as they were told, for they knew better than to mess with the sheriff.

Lane and Rick watched as they grabbed Mose by the arms to drag him from the saloon.

Only when Mose had been removed from the saloon did Lane finally holster his gun. He looked at the sheriff. "Thanks."

The lawman nodded to him as he, too, holstered his gun. "No, thank you. We don't need killers like him running loose in our town."

Rick handed over Mose's gun to the sheriff, and then the lawman left them to see about locking the prisoner up.

Rick looked at Lane. "I could use a drink. What about you?"

Lane said nothing as he joined his friend at the bar and ordered a whiskey. The trek to find Mose had been long and hard, but it had been worth it. He took a deep drink of the potent liquor and wondered if he could go back to ranching after all that had happened.

Chapter One

Three Years Later
Black Rock, Texas

It was late on a hot summer night, and the mood was wild in the Tumbleweed Saloon. The notorious outlaw Dan Cooper and his gang had ridden into town earlier that afternoon. They'd robbed a stagecoach the week before and had gotten clean away. They'd come to Black Rock looking for a good time, and they'd found it there at the Tumbleweed. They had been drinking and gambling and enjoying the company of the buxom saloon girls, who were eager to please the free-spending outlaws.

It wasn't often that Dan and his men could relax and let their guard down this way, but in Black Rock the sheriff, Hal Brown, was a known coward. They'd had a few run-ins with him in the past, and he'd learned to make himself scarce whenever the Cooper Gang showed up.

Dan Cooper wasn't a big man, but there was an edge of danger about him—about the way he held himself and the way he wore his gun—that made him an imposing figure as he sat at the table, drinking his whiskey and playing poker.

The red-haired saloon girl Lila wasn't afraid of Dan, though. She'd been with him in the past and couldn't wait to get him upstairs again.

"What do you think, Big Dan?" Lila purred enticingly as she came to stand close beside him. "You gonna win this hand and come upstairs with me? I'm tired of waiting."

Dan was well aware that Lila was very talented at pleasing a man. He'd partaken of her services many times before during visits to the Tumbleweed, and he enjoyed being with her, but right then he had to concentrate on playing out his hand. "You bet I am. Just stay right here with me and bring me some good luck."

"You know I will," she whispered seductively.

Dan turned his full attention back to the poker game, taking care to keep his expression carefully guarded as he studied the cards he held in his hand. This had been a good night for him. The winnings piled high on the table before him were proof of that, and he was certain his luck was only going to get better. Lifting his gaze, he looked over at the two men sitting at the table with him and saw their tense expressions. Dan smiled to himself, for he knew they wouldn't be sitting there much longer—not with the hand he was holding now.

"I'll raise you," he said in a calm, even tone, determined to take them for all he could. He enjoyed the look of shock on the other gamblers' faces when he pushed all of his cash to the center of the table.

"What—?" Will Taylor, the local blacksmith, was angry.

"You heard me," Dan said arrogantly.

Even though he had two pairs, Will knew there was no way he could match Dan's bet. Barely controlling his disgust at losing all his money, he threw in his hand and shoved his chair back away from the table. "I'm out."

Dan turned to Chuck Davis. He didn't know Chuck well. They'd just met for the first time that day. Chuck was just passing through town and had come in for a drink, then ended up in the game.

"What about you?" Dan asked.

Chuck kept his cards close to his chest as he looked over at Dan. He'd always considered himself a good poker player, but it was hard for him to tell if the other man was bluffing or not. Chuck glanced back down at the three nines he'd been dealt and believed he held the winning hand. He counted out what money he had left in front of him and then looked up again to meet Dan's cold-eyed stare. "I'm low on cash, but I can bet my ranch."

"How big a ranch you got?" he challenged.

"The Circle D is big enough to match your bet," he replied firmly. He knew better than to show any sign of weakness around a man like Dan Cooper.

"Where is this ranch of yours?"

"Over near Bluff Springs."

Dan nodded as he considered the offer. He looked back down at his own cards.

The saloon had suddenly gone quiet as everyone realized just how tense the game had become. The stakes were high—real high if this Chuck Davis was betting his ranch. The other customers gathered around the table to see which gambler was going to win.

"You must be feeling mighty good about your hand," Dan sneered, giving the rancher a smug grin.

"I am," Chuck replied evenly, but inwardly, he was bristling at the outlaw's arrogance. He didn't let his irritation show, though, for he'd heard how dangerous this man and his gang were, and he didn't want to get caught up in a shoot-out. He just wanted to win all the money that was riding on this game. He'd been going through some hard times on the Circle D and needed the cash to keep the place going. "What do you say?"

"I've always wanted to be a rancher."

"Well, let's see what you've got," Chuck challenged.

Dan smiled confidently as he slowly spread his full

house of kings and tens out on the tabletop for all to see. "What are you holding?"

For a moment, Chuck could only stare at the other man's winning hand in disbelief, and then the reality of what had happened hit him. He'd lost everything. Slowly, painfully, he tossed his losing hand on the table.

"Whoo-hooo!" Dan roared. "Looks like Lila here brought me all that good luck she was promising!"

A roar went through the crowd as Dan got up and kissed the saloon girl hotly before swinging her around in celebration.

"What do you say, boys? Looks like I just got me a ranch! I'm buying! Drinks are on me!" Dan stood up and raked in all the money he'd just won. He stuffed his pockets full of the cash. "We got some celebrating to do." He looked over at Chuck. "I'll find you later, and we'll talk."

Chuck only nodded.

Dan turned away from the table, and, keeping Lila at his side, he headed to the bar to join his men.

"You just had yourself one lucky night," drawled Seth Rawlins, the fastest gun in the gang.

"Yes, I did," Dan agreed, picking up the glass of whiskey the bartender had set before him. He took a deep drink as he eyed Lila hungrily and then grinned. "And the night's not over yet."

"No, it's not," Seth said, leering at Lila.

The other three members of the gang, Ted Wilkins,

John Harris and Al Meade, who went by the nickname of Slick, came over to congratulate Dan.

"That sure was a fine hand," John told him.

"I'll say," Dan agreed.

"What are you going to do with the ranch?" Ted asked.

"Why, I'm going to settle down—maybe get me a wife and have some kids," Dan joked.

They all laughed, for they knew what kind of man he really was.

Dan was laughing with them.

"I'll think of something," he assured him. "But right now, I got something else on my mind—"

Two of the other saloon girls came over to him, a buxom blonde known as Francie and a dark-haired beauty named Dolly.

"I love a winner," Francie said brazenly, positioning herself close enough to him so he could have a clear view of her cleavage in her low-cut dress.

"So do I," Dolly agreed.

Dan eyed them both, but he knew Lila had more to offer him—a lot more. "I've already got the woman I need." He looked brazenly down the front of Lila's gown. "But some of my boys will be glad to show you a good time. Won't you, boys?"

"You bet," Seth replied.

Seth quickly grabbed Francie and yanked her over to him while Slick went after Dolly.

"Lila, darling, you done got yourself a winner tonight." Dan smiled at her. "Let's go upstairs and get this celebration started!"

Lila took his arm and drew him up the staircase and down the hall to her room in the back. Dan had won big tonight, and she knew he was going to take care of her real good.

Francie looked up at Seth. "What about you? Are you ready for a good time now that the gambling's over?"

"The gambling's not over," Seth said, trying not to smile.

"What are you talking about?" Francie was becoming frustrated in her efforts to get him upstairs, and she was confused by his statement. "The big game is over. There's no more betting going on."

"Sure there is, woman." He chuckled at her. "I'm betting you're going to entertain me real nice."

Francie smiled enticingly. "I'd say that was a safe bet on your part, and I raise you—"

"By how much?"

"Come on. I'll have to show you how much—" She started toward the staircase, giving him an inviting look.

Seth's gaze was heated as he set his drink aside and went after her. "I think I'm going to enjoy playing this hand."

Francie looked over her shoulder as she mounted the steps ahead of him. "No doubt about it."

Slick wasted no time taking Dolly to one of the empty tables at the back of the room, while John and Ted returned to the bar. At that moment, they were more interested in drinking than womanizing.

It was almost closing time when Seth came downstairs to the saloon again and found Dan sitting at a table near the back of the room. The crowd had thinned out, so Seth got himself another drink from the bar and went to sit with the outlaw leader.

"This has been a great night," Seth said as he settled in, leaning back in his chair to relax.

"So Francie took good care of you?"

"Oh, yeah. She earned her money." He was feeling unusually satisfied. Francie had tried to resist him at the start, claiming he was being too rough, but she'd shut up after he'd shown her what 'rough' really was. She'd smartened up then and hadn't given him any more trouble. He liked roughing up women. The violence touched something in him that sex alone could not.

Dan paused to draw his full attention. "Seth, I've been thinking about this ranch I just won."

Seth chuckled. "What did you decide? You really are gonna take up ranching, settle down now? Maybe even get yourself a wife?"

"No. I'm not, but I was thinking maybe you were."

Seth frowned. "What are you talking about? What have you got in mind?"

Dan quickly explained, "We've been needing a safe place to hide out whenever the law comes after us, and what better place than—"

"The Circle D," Seth finished.

"It's a good ride from here. It's over by Bluff Springs." Dan nodded. "You could show up there as the new owner. You're not as well-known as I am. There wouldn't be too many questions asked. Why, you could even send back East for one of them mail-order brides. She'd have no idea what was going on, and you'd look like a real upstanding citizen when you settled in, got yourself a wife, and took over running things."

They shared a knowing look.

"And no one would ever suspect it was our hideout," Seth finished.

"That's right," Dan said with great satisfaction, thinking his plan was perfect. "And every now and then you could take a 'trip' and ride with us."

"I'd like that. I'd like that a lot." Seth enjoyed their dangerous lifestyle. He liked that people were frightened when they heard the Cooper Gang was coming. It made him feel strong, and if he was living right there in the middle of law-abiding citizens and they didn't know who he was, he was going to enjoy being an outlaw even more.

"Good, we'll do it. I already talked to Chuck. He was still here waiting for me when I came back down.

The Circle D is mine, but as far as the ranch hands are concerned—I told him to send word that Seth Rawlins was the new owner, and Chuck knows better than to say any different."

The two men were quiet for a moment as each took a deep drink. Then Seth looked up and grinned.

"Well, Boss, I guess if I'm going to be 'settling down,' first thing in the morning I'd better see about sending a telegram to get me one of those brides. Some little girl is going to get real lucky coming out here to marry me."

The two men laughed and continued their drinking, unaware that the saloon girl Dolly was sitting at a table nearby and had overheard their every word.

Chapter Two

Two Days Later

It was getting late in the afternoon. Several of the townsfolk stopped what they were doing and turned to watch as a tall, lean, dark-haired stranger rode slowly down the main street of town. The lone rider looked like trouble to them, and because gunmen came often to Black Rock, they knew they should get off the street. The shooting could start up at any time.

Texas Ranger Lane Madison was aware that people were watching him, but he didn't care. He kept his gaze focused straight ahead as he continued on toward the saloon.

He was a man on a mission, and he had only one thing on his mind.

He had come to town to track down the Cooper Gang.

Lane had been in Black Rock once before, several years ago, and it was obvious things had changed since then. The town looked even more run-down now. He knew the place had a sheriff named Brown, but from what he'd heard, the lawman was useless against the big guns. Lane intended to seek him out and have a talk with him about Dan Cooper and his men, but first he wanted to stop at the saloon and get a feel for the place.

Catching sight of the Tumbleweed Saloon, Lane reined in out front and dismounted. He tied up his horse and then paused for a moment to look around. The street seemed quiet enough, so he went on inside. The place was reasonably crowded. There were poker games going on at the tables and several men drinking at the bar. Lane joined those standing in front of the polished oak bar.

Lane had deliberately taken off his Ranger badge before he'd ridden into town. He wanted to remain anonymous while he was in the saloon in the hope that the talk going on around him would be more open.

Harold, the bartender, had seen him come in and went to wait on him. "What can I get you?"

"Whiskey," Lane answered.

Harold made short order of pouring him a stiff drink. "You just passing through, or you planning to stay around for a while?"

"I'm not sure."

Harold was used to that kind of answer. "Well, if you need another drink, just holler."

"I will," Lane said, paying him for the whiskey.

Lane picked up his glass and took a deep drink. The last information he'd been given about Dan Cooper and his gang of killers was that they had been thought to be riding for Black Rock after robbing a stage. That meant they would have been here some time in the past two weeks.

It wasn't often Lane let his emotions drive him, but after he'd learned what the cold-blooded outlaws had done during the robbery, he'd known he had to bring them in. Not only had they shot the stage driver, but in the hail of gunfire that had followed, a young mother and her four-year-old daughter had also been killed. Now, he was in Black Rock, hoping to learn something that would help him pick up their trail.

Lila was in the back of the saloon flirting with all the gamblers. She wasn't having any luck distracting them from their games, so she decided to go after the new man who'd just walked in.

Even from this distance Lila could tell he was one fine-looking man. She cast a quick glance at the gamblers at the table. They were nothing but ugly drunks, and she knew she was ready for a change. This tall, handsome man was just what she needed, and she set her sights on him.

"Welcome to the Tumbleweed," Lila purred, coming

up behind him as he stood at the bar. Her gaze lingered on the broad, powerful width of his shoulders.

Lane heard the saloon girl's greeting and turned to find the scantily dressed female standing behind him, eyeing him with interest, her expression openly seductive. "Afternoon," he returned.

"I'm Lila."

"Nice to meet you, Lila." Lane thought she might be just the one he needed to talk to.

"You, too. What's your name?" she asked in a sultry tone.

"Lane Madison," he answered.

"Well, Lane Madison, what brings you to the Tumbleweed? You looking for a good time, or did you just need a drink?"

"I'm always looking for a good time," he told her.

"Well, you've found it."

"That's good to hear. Can I buy you a drink?"

"I'd like that," Lila accepted eagerly.

Harold quickly served her and then moved away again once he'd been paid.

Lila took a sip of her drink and gazed up at Lane. By the time she'd finished the glass, she realized that despite several minutes of flirtation, she knew little more about the stranger than when she'd met him. She was trying her best to get him upstairs when the shouts broke out at the back of the room.

Lane had been playing along with her, biding his time when the fight started.

The bartender started cussing loudly as the violence erupted.

Lane glanced over at him just as Harold picked up the shotgun he kept hidden behind the bar and went out to put a stop to the brawl.

"I think we'd better step back a little," Lane told her, drawing her away from the ruckus.

She didn't hesitate to go with him.

They stayed at the end of the bar that was farthest away from the trouble and watched as Harold brought the fight under control. The bartender was a tough man, and the men who were fighting knew it. When he stalked up with his shotgun and ordered them out of the bar, all but one of the men involved stopped fighting. When that man started to pick up a chair to throw at someone, the bartender hit him on the head with his shotgun.

"Get him out of here!" Harold bellowed in disgust as he stood over the fallen man.

Harold watched angrily, shotgun still in hand, as several of those involved in the brawl dragged the unconscious gambler from the saloon and threw him in the street. Only when they were gone did Harold return to the bar and put his gun away.

"Good job, Harold," Lila said calmly. She was accustomed to the ugly side of saloon life and knew a strong hand was necessary to keep things under control. Early on, Harold had actually had to use his shotgun to restore order in the Tumbleweed. These days, his reputation was so well-known that very few ever dared to challenge him. No one wanted to push Harold too far.

Harold gave a shake of his head as he looked over at her. "If they can't afford to lose, they shouldn't be gambling. That ol' boy is stupid. He only lost a few hundred. When was it? Just a few nights ago a fella lost his whole ranch in a poker game, and he didn't start no fight."

"Of course he didn't start no fight," Dolly put in, joining their conversation as she strutted up to the bar. When the fight had broken out, she'd hurried away from the drunks to hide out until everything quieted down. Now that the saloon was quiet again, she wanted to find out more about the man Lila was flirting with. "He would have ended up dead if he had."

Lane heard her statement and wondered if he was on to something. "Why is that?" He looked at the bartender. "I've seen you in action. You could have broken up a fight if one started."

"Those gamblers were different," Dolly explained. "The man who won is known for being real mean—and real fast on the draw. The loser was lucky he walked away, even if it was with just the clothes on his back."

"Do you know who the gunman was?" Lane asked, looking between the bartender and the ladies.

"Just one of the wild ones who pass through here sometimes," Harold answered quickly, giving the girls a censoring look that told them to keep their mouths shut.

Lane knew what the bartender was doing by giving the girls that look, and now he believed even more that he was on the right trail. The Cooper Gang had been to the Tumbleweed Saloon.

"There are a lot more losers than winners in a poker game," Harold said.

"You're right about that," Lane agreed with a half smile. "I learned that lesson a long time ago."

Lila looked up at him and purred seductively, "You don't look like a 'loser' to me, handsome."

Lane chuckled and smiled down at her. "Why, thank you, Lila. You just got yourself another drink. Give the lady whatever she wants." He tossed some more money on the bar for the bartender.

"I'll tell you what I want—" she began as she leaned closer to him, wanting his full attention.

"I'll tell you what I want, too," Dolly put in quickly, ignoring Lila's testy look as she interrupted. When the stranger glanced her way, something about him seemed different from the other men.

Lane was surprised that the pretty, dark-haired girl was flirting with him, too, but he wasn't interested in her either. He had to talk to the sheriff and find out if Dan Cooper had been the deadly gunman who'd been in town, and if so, where the outlaw had been headed when he'd left Black Rock. "I appreciate your offers, ladies, but I have to be going."

Lila was not used to rejection. She was shocked and a bit insulted by his dismissal. "I can show you a real good time—and I can make it fast. Just ask any of the boys. They'll tell you."

"Some other time, maybe," he said easily.

He finished off the last of his drink, and, nodding to the two saloon girls, he walked out of the Tumbleweed, leaving the women staring after him in frustration.

Lila picked up her newly refilled glass and glared at Dolly. "You didn't have to come over here."

"You don't get first pick of all the handsome ones," she retorted.

Lila just turned and strutted away to where the gamblers were starting up a new game. She had to get back to work. Only one good thing had come out of spending time with Lane Madison: he'd bought her a few drinks, and the more she drank, the better the other men looked to her.

Dolly stayed at the bar and frowned a little as she looked at Harold.

"Who was that man?" she asked.

"He said his name was Lane Madison. Why?"

"I don't know. There was just something about him—He's not like a lot of the other men we get in here."

"Maybe you've done business with him in the past," Harold suggested.

"Oh, no," Dolly quickly protested. "If I had gotten him upstairs, I would have remembered every minute of it."

Meanwhile in St. Louis

Bryce Parker never forgot a man who owed him a debt, and Raymond Howard was heavily indebted to him. As he heard Howard's carriage pull up in front of his home, he smiled confidently.

The moment he'd been waiting for had arrived.

Raymond Howard was there.

Bryce smiled broadly to himself and remained seated until the maid knocked on the door.

"Mr. Parker? Raymond Howard is here to see you," the girl announced.

"See him in," Bryce responded. He turned serious as he got to his feet to welcome his visitor. Bryce watched Raymond walk into the study, and he noticed how the other man eyed his opulent surroundings. Bryce felt very proud that he had Raymond right where he wanted him.

"Good afternoon, Bryce," Raymond offered, struggling to keep his manner confident. He knew what a predator Bryce was and didn't want to appear weak.

"We have much to discuss," Bryce Parker began, getting straight down to business as he came around the desk. He did not offer to shake his visitor's hand but gestured toward the chair in front of his desk. "Have a seat."

Raymond sat down and couldn't help feeling intimidated when the other man remained standing. Just knowing that Bryce had outmaneuvered him left him outraged. The knowledge that there was nothing he could do about it made him even more frustrated and furious.

Bryce leaned a hip casually against his desk as he confronted Raymond. "In the course of our business dealings, you have come to owe me a considerable amount of money."

"I'm well aware of that," Raymond replied tersely.

"Good, I'm glad you're aware of what you owe, because the time has come for you to pay up."

Raymond had suspected that was the reason Bryce had insisted upon this private meeting here at his home. "As I told you, I am working at finding a way to repay you."

"I'm afraid 'working at finding a way' isn't enough, Raymond," Bryce said, piercing the other man with a cold-eyed look. "I am a businessman. I want my money now."

Desperation took hold of Raymond. Bryce had a reputation for dealing harshly with anyone who crossed him, and he'd heard more than a few stories of what a dangerous enemy he could be. He certainly didn't want to turn Bryce into an enemy. "I'll need more time—" he began.

Bryce cut him off before he could say another word. "You're out of time, Raymond. I am not a patient man."

"But there's nothing I can do to access the funds. The money is tied up in my dead wife's estate. There's no way I can completely settle my debt until—"

"Yes, there is."

"There is? What?" Raymond asked in frightened confusion.

"You have something I want . . ." Bryce deliberately left the sentence hanging. He liked having control over the other man.

"I do?" Raymond was startled by the younger man's declaration, and he couldn't imagine what he was talking about.

"That's right. You do, and I intend to get it."

"What is it? Name it. Whatever I have—is yours—" He was frantic to find a way to pay off his debt to Bryce. If he got through this, Raymond knew in the future he would not be so foolhardy in his dealings anymore.

Bryce turned a threatening regard on the weakling sitting before him. "I want Destiny."

"Destiny—" Shock hammered through Raymond at the mention of his stepdaughter.

"Yes. She's going to marry me."

In that instant, Raymond realized what Bryce was about. Bryce's reputation was known far and wide. Whenever he wanted something, he got it, and he'd been wanting to be accepted by the upper echelon of St. Louis society for some time now. Few in society paid much attention to Bryce, though, for despite his success in business, he came from a family with no social status. By marrying Destiny, Bryce would accomplish his goal. The Sterling family was one of the most highly regarded in the area. Raymond himself had certainly benefited from the Sterling's connections when he'd married the widowed Annabelle.

"That's right. As soon as Destiny becomes my bride, all your debts will be forgiven."

Desperate as he was, Raymond was determined to make the marriage happen. "How do you want to handle this?"

"Bring her here to me tonight—at, say, seven o'clock."

"Should I tell her of your intentions?"

"Do whatever you want to do. Just make sure she's here with me tonight—unchaperoned." Bryce felt the heat rise in his body as he said the last. He was definitely looking forward to the evening to come.

Raymond stood up and started from the study. "She'll be here."

"Don't be late."

His words weren't a suggestion.

They were an order—and a threat.

Lane had taken the time to look around town. He couldn't quite put his finger on what it was, but something seemed a little off. The place was too quiet, as if the townspeople felt threatened by some unnamed danger. Could it be the Cooper Gang? Had Black Rock recently been visited by the killers? He hoped the sheriff would have answers to some of his questions.

When he reached the office, he glanced in the window and saw the sheriff sitting at his desk, so he opened the door and strode in.

Sheriff Brown looked up quickly, and a bit nervously, as the stranger unexpectedly entered his office. There was an edge of danger about the tall, dark-haired man standing there just inside the doorway, and he wondered who he was and what he wanted.

"Evening." Sheriff Brown hurried to his feet. "What can I do for you?"

For a moment, Lane just stared at the dark-haired, mustachioed weasel of a man wearing the sheriff's badge. Sizing the fellow up, he could guess what a poor excuse for a lawman he was. Ever so slowly, Lane took his own badge out of his pocket and pinned it on his shirt.

"I'm Ranger Lane Madison, and I'm here on business."

Sheriff Brown's eyes widened at the news, and he swallowed tightly as he stared at the imposing figure standing before him. It was no wonder he'd thought the stranger looked dangerous. He was—this man was a Texas Ranger.

"What brings you to Black Rock, Ranger Madison?" he asked quickly. "Things have been real quiet around here lately."

Lane ignored him and got straight down to business.

"I'm after the Cooper Gang," he answered tersely.

"The Cooper Gang?" the lawman repeated, suddenly sounding more than a little unsettled.

"That's right." Lane watched the sheriff carefully, judging his reaction. "I've been tracking the killer Dan Cooper and his men, and I have reason to believe they were headed this way. I wondered if you had seen or heard anything of them over the last week or so?"

"No, no, I haven't heard a thing," Brown quickly denied, "and I surely would have known if they were anywhere around here—"

"Are you certain?" Lane pressed. Judging from the way the sheriff was acting, Lane had no doubt the man was a coward—and a liar.

"Yeah, yeah, I'm certain."

Lane's disgust with the man grew. Lawmen were supposed to be brave, to protect their towns even at the risk of their own lives, not run and hide at the first sign of trouble. "I was just down at the Tumbleweed, and I heard talk there that there were some bad boys in town a few days ago."

"There was no one here causing any trouble. It's been real quiet this week," Brown denied.

"Well, if you do happen to hear anything about the gang's whereabouts, or if you remember anything that I should be aware of, let me know. I'll be staying here in town at the hotel tonight."

"I'm not going to remember anything about any gunfighters," Sheriff Brown told him heatedly, growing angry and more uneasy at the Ranger's arrogant ways. He drew himself up straight as he glared at the other man. "Because there isn't anything to remember."

Lane nodded and turned to leave the office. He wasn't quite sure what was going on in Black Rock, but it seemed like a lot of folks in this town had something to hide, and he was going to find out what it was.

Lane got his horse from where he'd left it tied up in front of the saloon and then went to take a room at the hotel.

Chapter Three

Sheriff Brown was shaking in his boots at the thought of having a Texas Ranger right there in his town. He watched until Ranger Madison had moved out of sight and then left his office to head down to the Tumbleweed. He hurried up to the bar and ordered a stiff drink.

"What's the matter, Sheriff?" Harold asked, puzzled by the lawman's frightened behavior. There were no outlaws or dangerous gunmen in town tonight, so he had no idea why the man was acting so scared. "Something troubling you?"

"Oh, yeah," Sheriff Brown said, downing most of his drink in one big swallow and then shoving the nearly empty glass back at the barkeep for a quick refill.

Harold obliged and then waited as the sheriff drank most of the second shot.

"There's a Texas Ranger in town, and he's looking

for the Cooper Gang," Brown finally managed to choke out.

Harold tensed. "Is his name Madison?"

"Yeah, that's his name. Lane Madison."

Harold swore under his breath. "I was wondering what he was up to, and now I know. So, he's after Dan and the boys, is he?"

"That's right."

"He's going to need a lot of luck, going up against them."

"If he ever finds them. You didn't tell him anything, did you?"

"No, not a word."

"Good," Brown said shakily. "We don't need Dan getting all mad and coming back here hell-bent on revenge, you know."

"Don't worry. That Ranger didn't learn anything from us. If he's going to find Dan, he'll have to do it on his own."

Dolly had finally been able to entice one of the men to accompany her upstairs, and she was just passing by the bar with him when she overheard most of Harold's conversation with the sheriff. Her reaction to Lane Madison earlier made sense to her now. He was a Texas Ranger. He was a good man. She knew right then she had to find a way to talk to the Ranger again that night. She would slip away to the hotel and tell him everything she knew about what had gone on with Dan Cooper and his men. Dolly was sure if anyone could bring down the Cooper Gang, it was Ranger Madison.

"You ready for a good time, honey?" her cowboy asked, sweeping her up in his arms to charge up the steps with her.

"I sure am," she assured him with a bright smile, but her thoughts were elsewhere as they disappeared down the upstairs hall to her room.

Raymond had ensconced himself in his study for the afternoon, but his thoughts were upstairs with his stepdaughter, Destiny. He had to figure out how best to put Bryce's proposition to her. It wasn't going to be easy. She was as headstrong and difficult as her mother had been.

Destiny's strong will aside, Raymond could understand why Bryce wanted her. Not only would she help him socially, but she was a beautiful young woman with stunning blonde hair and a curvaceous figure. Living in the family's home with her as he did, there wasn't a day that he didn't think about taking her. He'd managed to control himself so far, and, now, considering Bryce's demands, it was a good thing that he had. She was still untouched, and that was important. He had to deliver unsullied goods to Bryce.

The more he thought about it, the more he liked

the idea of marrying her off to Bryce, for once his debts had been forgiven, he could start living life the way he'd always wanted to now that Annabelle was dead. Yes, it was time to let his stepdaughter know what the future held in store for her.

Destiny answered her stepfather's summons accompanied by Sylvia, the maid who'd become her closest confidante since her mother's death.

"You wanted to see me?" Destiny asked Raymond as she joined him.

Sylvia had told her he had insisted on speaking to her and was waiting for her in his study.

"Yes." He looked up to see the maid still standing by the hallway door. "Sylvia, you may go," he ordered.

The maid slipped quietly away, but she was frowning as she disappeared down the hall. She couldn't help wondering what Raymond was up to.

In the past eight months since Miss Annabelle's death from the fever, she'd been very protective of Destiny. As a longtime faithful servant of the Sterling family, she'd never liked or trusted her mistress's second husband. She'd known why Miss Annabelle had married him—Raymond was good-looking and charming, and Miss Annabelle had been vulnerable after Mr. Sterling's death, but once they'd married, the truth about his character had slowly come out, and it hadn't been pretty. Sylvia hurried on into the kitchen, more than a little unsettled by the way Raymond was acting this afternoon.

Alone with Destiny, Raymond faced her. He was ready for the challenge to come. He expected resistance from her, but he was prepared to deal with any and all of her arguments. "We haven't really had a conversation about this before, but as your stepfather, it is my obligation to see to your future."

Destiny was instantly alert at his words. Something about Raymond had always troubled her. When he'd married her mother, she'd been forced to accept him as family, but she had never ever thought of him as a father figure. There was something about him that always left her uneasy, and, since her mother's passing, she'd become even more uncomfortable around him. "My future? What are you talking about?"

Destiny had made her debut the previous fall and had had a few ardent suitors calling on her, but when her mother had passed away shortly thereafter, she had gone into mourning and hadn't been seeing anyone socially for a time now.

"You're eighteen now, and it's time for you to marry," Raymond pronounced in his most imperious tone.

She was shocked by his statement. "But I'm not in love with anyone—"

"The idea that 'love' should be the foundation of a marriage is hardly the truth of life, my dear," he sneered. "Marriage is far more than that."

"I don't understand." She was confused by his harsh tone and didn't know what he was talking about.

"Bryce Parker has expressed an interest in marrying you—"

"What?" She barely knew Bryce Parker, although she had heard some talk of his ruthless business exploits in town.

"Bryce has asked me for your hand in marriage, and I've agreed to the union. I've arranged for you to see him tonight at his home. If all goes well, the wedding will take place as soon as possible."

"What?" She was shocked. "You're out of your mind—" Unconsciously, Destiny took a step back, away from her stepfather. "I'm not marrying Bryce Parker or anyone else right now. I'm still in mourning for my mother."

"Your mother's been dead for an eternity!" he snarled. "Get over it."

"Like you have?" she challenged.

"That's right. Your mother is not coming back!" And in his thoughts, he was very glad about that.

"How can you talk this way about her? It's only been eight months since—"

"Are you counting every day?" he derided. "It's time for you to put the past behind you and to start thinking about your future. That's exactly what I've been doing, and that's why I've decided you can do no better than to marry a man as rich and successful as Bryce."

"You're crazy! I'm not going to marry Bryce Parker! I won't—You can't make me!"

Raymond took a step toward her in a threatening move that was meant to cow her. "Au contraire, my dear. I am the head of this household, and you will do exactly what I tell you to do. You will meet with Bryce this evening, and you will accept his proposal of marriage. Do you understand me?"

"You can't tell me what to do!" Destiny glared up at him.

Raymond smiled coldly at her as he grabbed her tightly by the arm and sneered, "Oh, but I can. I am your guardian, and as such, you will do as I say."

Destiny struggled to pull away from him. "My mother may have married you, but you're nothing to me! You never have been, and you never will be!"

He tightened his hold on her even more and felt a thrill of power at her squirming. Even so, he was careful not to bruise her. He couldn't risk delivering damaged goods to Bryce that evening. That would never do. Raymond gave her a slight shake.

"Let me put it to you this way, my dear," he began, leering openly at her. "You can marry Bryce, or . . ."

Destiny waited, unsure of what he was going to say next.

"Or you can marry me."

Destiny froze, and her eyes widened in horror at the thought as she stared up at him. She saw the lust in his eyes and knew everything she had ever suspected about him was true.

Raymond was a horrible man!

She'd long believed he'd used her mother, marrying her only for the money, and now she knew she'd been right.

Destiny swallowed nervously. Her mind was racing as she tried to figure a way out of this. As repugnant as the idea of marrying Bryce was to her, she knew there was only one thing she could do to escape her stepfather. For now, she had to pretend to agree to his terms. Then once she managed to get away from him, she would find a way out of the marriage.

She looked at him in complete disgust as she replied, "All right, that made my decision much easier. What time do I have to be ready to leave to meet Bryce?"

Her words were like a harsh slap in the face to Raymond. He was so angered by her attitude, he wanted to backhand her. It took a major effort on his part, but he controlled himself.

"Bryce is expecting you at seven. Be ready."

He let her go and watched as she quickly backed away from him.

"Don't worry. I will be."

Destiny fled to the safety of her room and locked

the door behind her. She stood there uncertainly, staring around herself, trying to figure out what to do next. She was desperate.

How had this happened?

How had Raymond gotten such control over her life?

Her mother had taught her to be bold and to stand up for herself, and she had. She had refused to show any fear before Raymond—but now, alone in her room, tears welled up in her eyes.

A soft tap at the door startled Destiny, and she spun around and took a step backward, fearing Raymond had come after her.

"Who is it?" she asked nervously.

"It's me—Sylvia—Are you all right?" the servant asked, her voice just above a whisper so Raymond wouldn't hear her. She, too, knew how dominating and controlling he could be.

Destiny wasted no time unlocking the door to admit the maid, then quickly closed it again.

Sylvia could see the haunted look in Destiny's eyes, and she knew something was terribly wrong. "What did Mr. Howard do to you?"

"He gave me two choices—" she answered in an emotion-choked voice.

"Choices?" Sylvia repeated in a confused tone.

Destiny nodded. "He says I can marry Bryce Parker—"

The maid was shocked.

"Or—" She paused.

"Or what?"

Destiny swallowed nervously as she met the older woman's gaze. "Or I can marry him."

"Oh, dear God," the servant muttered in absolute disgust. "You can't marry your stepfather!"

"I know," she agreed wholeheartedly, shuddering at the thought.

"What are you going to do?"

"He's already arranged for me to see Bryce tonight. I'm supposed to be ready to go to Bryce's house at seven o'clock."

"I've heard talk about him. They say he's good-looking and rich. Do you want to marry him?"

Destiny looked up at Sylvia, her expression troubled. "I know he's rich and handsome as you said, but I don't love him—I don't even know him that well. I've only met him a few times."

The maid touched her arm to reassure her. She could just imagine how very alone and lost Destiny must be feeling. "Just because you're going to see Bryce Parker tonight, doesn't mean you have to marry him tonight. Your mother certainly wouldn't have let you rush into a marriage."

Destiny felt a ray of hope for the first time. "Maybe there's some way out of this—"

"We can try to think of something."

"Yes, but I can't let Raymond know."

"You're right about that," Sylvia said, her disgust with the man obvious in her voice.

"You don't like him either?"

"I never have," Sylvia said with conviction. "I don't trust him. If you need me to help you in any way, I'll do it."

"Thank you." Destiny knew Sylvia was the only person she could count on anymore, the only person she could trust.

Sylvia gave Destiny a quick, loving hug and then left her to herself to get ready for the evening ahead.

Lane got cleaned up and ate dinner at the hotel before going back to the saloon for the evening. He was going to play some poker tonight in the hope that someone might start talking about the big card game that had happened when the gunmen were in town. This time as he went into the saloon, though, he was wearing his badge.

"I was wondering if you'd come back in tonight, Ranger Madison," Harold said, giving him a smile as he walked into the saloon.

Finding out that those in the bar already knew his true identity even before they'd seen him wearing his badge made Lane all the more determined to pay close attention to everything that went on in the Tumbleweed tonight.

"I got my work taken care of, and now I can relax for a while," he responded.

If this town was trying to protect the gang in any way, Lane was determined to bring them all down. Now that his identity was known as well as his reason for being in Black Rock, he would have to be even more careful than before, in case the gang was nearby and had been alerted to his presence. He went to join a poker game at the far end of the room and sat with his back to the wall so he could watch everything that was going on around him. He didn't want any surprises tonight.

Chapter Four

The carriage ride to Bryce Parker's mansion seemed endless as Destiny stared blankly out the window. She was trying to ignore Raymond, who was seated across from her, but he was making it impossible with his incessant talking.

"This will be a very smart marriage for you," he declared. "Bryce is wealthy and powerful. You'll want for nothing as his wife."

Destiny remained silent, although she had already decided to seek out her mother's attorney in the morning to see whether there was any way she could escape the dictates of Raymond's guardianship.

The carriage came to a stop in front of the two-story, elegant brick Parker mansion, and a servant immediately came out to help her down from the vehicle. As soon as Raymond had climbed out of the carriage after her, he took her by the arm and started up the walkway.

"Mr. Parker is expecting you," the doorman announced as he hurried ahead of them to hold the door open.

Bryce had enjoyed several brandies while he'd awaited Howard's return with Destiny. He was feeling most confident when the servant knocked on his study door to announce their arrival. He went out into the front hall to welcome them just as they walked in the door.

The sight of the beautiful Destiny standing right there before him, with her blonde hair done up in a sophisticated style and her lush curves clad in a modestly cut blue gown, sent a jolt of sensual heat through Bryce and left him eager to see her without the dress on. He smiled as he moved forward to speak with her.

"Good evening, Destiny," he greeted her warmly.

"Hello, Bryce," she returned, meeting the gaze of the tall, good-looking businessman. Darkly handsome though he was in his expensive, tailored suit, there was still something about him that left her feeling on edge.

Bryce greeted Raymond as a mere afterthought. "Raymond—I'm so glad you could join me this evening."

"Hello, Bryce," Raymond replied. "Thank you so much for your invitation. We're delighted to be here."

"Please, come in," Bryce directed, taking Destiny's arm and leading them into the dining room. "Dinner is almost ready."

Destiny had grown up in comfort, for the Sterling family was well-to-do, but the opulence of Bryce's home was far beyond anything she'd ever known. It was easy to tell from the ornate millwork, the crystal chandeliers, fine china and silverware, and the expensive furniture and rugs, that he was a man of vast wealth. It was also easy to tell that he wanted the whole world to know just how rich he was.

"Your home is lovely," she complimented him as he escorted her to a seat at the table just to the right of his own chair.

"Thank you, my dear," he returned. "I know your stepfather has been here several times before to visit, but I've never had the pleasure of your company before. I'll be glad to show you around later if you'd like."

As he and Raymond joined her at the table, the servants appeared and began to serve the meal. It was gourmet fare and quite delicious.

Destiny made only small talk throughout the meal. Most of the time, she just listened to the conversation between her stepfather and Bryce. She could tell things were a bit strained between them. She thought of Raymond's threat that if she didn't marry Bryce she would have to marry him, and she wondered what was really going on between the two men.

"The meal was delicious," Destiny offered as they finished the fancy chocolate dessert.

"I'm glad you enjoyed it."

"I did, too," Raymond said.

Bryce cast him a sidelong glance that let him know just how little he cared what Raymond thought.

Raymond got the message and quickly added, "Well, if you will excuse me now, I have to be on my way. I have some other business to take care of this evening."

"Of course," Bryce quickly agreed. He was more than happy to get the man out of his house so he could be alone with Destiny.

Destiny had no desire to be with Raymond, but she was surprised that he would leave her there unchaperoned with Bryce. "I guess I must be going, too."

"No, Destiny, you can stay here with Bryce and visit a little longer. I'll see you at home later," Raymond ordered.

Destiny was uneasy at the prospect but said nothing for the moment as Bryce got up and called for one of his servants.

"Please see Mr. Howard out and make sure Miss Sterling and I aren't disturbed for the rest of the evening."

"Yes, sir," the maid answered.

The two men bid each other good night, and the maid quickly ushered Raymond to the door. Once he was gone, Bryce turned his full attention back to Destiny.

"Come, my dear," Bryce invited. "Let's go into the parlor. I'm eager to get to know you better."

* * *

Lila was pouring on the charm tonight, but Lane had managed to put her off. Dolly had approached him, too, and he thought she seemed almost desperate in her attempts to get him to bed her, but he'd stayed at the poker table, winning some hands and losing some. Hours had passed, but Lane had learned nothing new listening to the talk around him. He decided it was time to call it a night and left the saloon with a little more money in his pocket for his efforts.

After he'd left the Tumbleweed, Lila went up to the bar to talk to Harold.

"You didn't have much luck with him tonight, did you, darling?" Harold teased her.

"Not with him I didn't. Let's just hope his luck is as bad as mine when he's trying to track Dan."

"Dan will be thanking you during his next trip through. I'll see to it."

"Thanks, Harold." She sighed wearily. "I think I'll turn in."

Dolly came up to the bar to join them. "I think I will, too. I'll see you both tomorrow."

They bid her good night, and Dolly left the Tumbleweed in her usual way. Once she was certain no one was following or watching her, she slipped off into a back alley and made her way to the hotel. She hid in the shadows behind the building, staring up at the windows to try to figure out which room was the Ranger's.

Chapter Five

Destiny was feeling increasingly uncomfortable as she sat on the sofa in Bryce's parlor, holding herself stiffly erect. She felt it was most inappropriate for her to be alone with a man she hardly knew, and she grew even more uncomfortable when he closed the hallway door behind them.

"Destiny, my dear, I must say you look absolutely ravishing tonight," Bryce said, trying to charm her. His gaze was openly hot upon her now that they were finally alone. Her fashionable gown was demure, but it only made him all the more determined to strip it from her. He wanted to bare those lush curves she was keeping hidden from him. "Would you care for a brandy?" he offered as he went to pour a snifter of brandy for himself.

"Oh, no. No, thank you," Destiny refused, trying to remember all the lessons her mother had given her about dealing with aggressive men. "It was nice of you to invite us over this evening."

"I've been looking forward to this moment for a long time," Bryce assured her, returning to sit down beside her. He gazed at her over the rim of the snifter as he took a drink of the potent liquor.

"Why is that?" Destiny felt he was sitting a bit too close to her, and he certainly had a strange look in his eyes, but, even so, she managed to give him a cordial smile.

Bryce wasted no time getting to the point. "Because I think you are a very beautiful young woman, and—I want to ask you to marry me."

"Oh—" She knew she shouldn't have been surprised that he had wasted no time getting to the point, but she was still caught a little off guard.

"I take it Raymond spoke to you about this?"

"Yes, he did mention it, but—"

"But what, my dear?" Bryce didn't understand why she wasn't thrilled by his proposal. This was the first time he'd ever proposed to a woman. He'd expected Destiny to be jumping up and down in excitement at the prospect of marrying him. Certainly, every other female in town would have been swooning at the possibility of being his bride and being in his bed. A slight edge of anger grew within him at her seeming lack of interest.

Destiny felt the aggressiveness in him, and she held herself very properly, her hands folded in her lap, the way her mother had always taught her. Then she looked him in the eye. She was hoping to put him off, to hold him at bay for a time, so she could figure out a way to escape this marriage Raymond had arranged for her. "But we barely know each other—"

"We can change that very quickly," he assured her, setting his snifter aside on a nearby table as he gave her a knowing smile.

"How can you be so sure you want to marry me?"

"Because I'm a man who always knows what he wants—and I want you," he answered arrogantly. "If we start planning the wedding now, we can be married in just a few months. We'll make sure our wedding is the social event of the season. That is, unless you'd like to elope tonight—"

"Bryce! Please—Stop it!" Destiny begged. "My mother died only recently. I'm still in mourning for her."

"I am sorry for your loss," he said, trying to sound sympathetic, but it was all an act. When he'd heard the news of Annabelle Sterling's death all those months before, he hadn't cared that the woman was dead. He'd only cared about Raymond losing access to the Sterling money and not being able to pay him back in full. Of course, in the end, everything had worked out just fine, because he'd figured out something he wanted from Raymond even more than money. "But it's time for you to think about your future—and together, I promise you, we will have a wonderful future—"

With nothing more to say, he made his move. He boldly took Destiny in his arms and kissed her, hungrily.

Lane had returned to his room and had started to get undressed. Even though the night had been peaceful so far, he was still feeling uneasy as he shrugged out of his shirt. Wanting to double-check, he'd taken one last look out the hotel room window, parting the curtains to stare down at the alley below. When he'd seen no sign of anyone moving around in the darkness, he'd let the curtains fall back down. Satisfied that all was quiet, he'd turned down the lamp. After putting his gun within reach on the small nightstand, he'd stretched out on the bed, ready to get some much needed sleep.

Dolly had been watching and waiting in the darkness, and she'd recognized Ranger Madison right away when he parted the curtains to take a look around—there was no mistaking that good-looking man, even from this distance. Once he'd closed the curtains again, she was ready to make her move. She'd slipped in the back door of the hotel. It was late, and there was no one around, so she'd had no trouble getting upstairs without being seen.

Lane was lying in bed, trying to relax, when he heard a sound out in the hallway by his door. It wasn't a loud noise. If it had been a drunk's raised voice or a door banging, he would have ignored it. What he heard sounded more like someone trying to sneak up on him, and he knew that could mean only trouble. Grabbing his gun, he moved silently to position himself by the door. He wasn't surprised when he saw the doorknob turn and the door slowly start to open.

Lane fully expected his unannounced visitor to be someone connected to the Cooper Gang, and he knew if it was, he would have to shoot first and ask questions later. He tensed as he saw the intruder's shadow on the floor, and his finger tightened on the trigger.

Dolly was frightened as she tried to slip into Lane's room undetected, but she knew she had to do this. She couldn't just knock on his door; she couldn't risk the possibility that someone else might hear her and the word would get out that she'd gone there to see him. She was moving as quietly as she could, for she didn't want anyone else in the hotel to know what she was doing. She had just about made it inside the door and was ready to whisper his name when she was suddenly grabbed by the arm and jerked bodily into the room.

"Don't! Bryce—stop!" Destiny exclaimed, pushing against his chest with all her might, trying to break away.

"I always knew you were a woman with spirit," he said, yanking her back tightly against him to kiss her again.

Destiny had been kissed by several of her suitors, but none of their embraces had been so forceful or so unwelcome. She continued to squirm, to try to get away from him, but his hold on her was too powerful, too controlling. Destiny knew in that moment what being married to Bryce would be like, and she knew she had to find a way to flee. When he touched her breast in a most inappropriate manner, she was startled, and she did something she'd never done before—she jerked one arm free and slapped him in the face as hard as she could.

"I said stop it!"

Bryce had believed her resistance was just a ploy to make him desire her even more, but when she slapped him, he'd had enough. No woman ever hit him and got away with it.

"So—you want to play rough, do you?" he ground out, drawing back to look down at her.

"What are you talking about? I want to go home!"

"This is what I'm talking about," he snarled.

Viciously, he backhanded her, and she cried out and collapsed on the sofa, stunned. Bryce pulled her fully beneath him then and ground his body suggestively against hers to let her know just how much he wanted her and what he planned to do to her.

"You're disgusting! Let me go!" Destiny recovered from the shock of his abuse and started to fight him again.

"Oh, no." He laughed. "We've only just begun."

"You're horrible! I'm not going to marry you!" she protested.

"Oh, yes, you are—" he sneered, reaching up to tear the neckline of her dress.

She gasped as he bared the tops of her breasts, and she continued to struggle to free herself from his vile touch.

"You're mine—your stepfather's sold you to me. You're not getting away from me—ever—" He bent his head and began to press hot, wet kisses across the tops of her breasts.

Destiny had never been touched this way before. Somehow she knew if she didn't escape from him now, she never would get away. Battling against his superior strength, she reached out to the table beside the sofa, groping around, hoping to find something—anything—she could use as a weapon.

Bryce was so intent on bringing Destiny to his will that she caught him totally by surprise when she managed to grab the vase that was on the table and bring it crashing down on the side of his head. The vase shattered on impact, and Bryce collapsed on top of her.

The struggle had only lasted a minute or so. Now Lane stood over his assailant, his gun trained on the dark figure as he quickly shut the door, locking it this time to make sure no one else could get in.

"Don't shoot!" Dolly begged him in a strangled voice as she found herself staring up at the barrel of his six-gun. In that instant, she knew what it was like to face death.

"What the—" Lane swore under his breath as he realized it was one of the saloon girls who was sprawled on the floor and not a member of the Cooper Gang. Furious that she'd put herself in such a dangerous situation, he grabbed her by the wrist and dragged her back up to her feet. "Don't move—" he snarled in a low voice as he made short order of lighting the lamp.

Dolly did as he'd ordered. She swallowed nervously as she waited to see what he was going to do.

Lane faced her, his gun still in hand. "What are you doing here?"

"I had to talk to you, but I couldn't do it at the saloon. I wanted to let you know what happened—"

"What are you talking about?"

"The Cooper gang—They were in town—" she began in a strangled voice.

The tension that had filled him began to ease, and he was suddenly worried about her safety. "Does anyone else know you're here? Did you tell anyone you were coming to talk to me?"

"No, I didn't tell anyone. I made sure no one knew. I came in through the alley. No one saw me."

Lane was glad she'd been that smart. He remained

silent for a second, realizing just how well she'd concealed herself in the alley. He hadn't seen her when he'd looked out, and knowing that he'd missed her left him disgusted with himself. He wouldn't make the mistake of being so careless again.

He motioned her toward the bed. "Sit down."

Dolly sat on the edge of his bed.

"Talk," he ordered as he holstered his gun. He was ready to listen to what she had to tell him.

She quickly explained everything she knew about the gang and what had happened when they visited the saloon. "I overheard Dan talking to Seth Rawlins. Dan won the Circle D, but Seth is going there to the ranch to pretend to be the new owner and take over running it. The gang is going to use it for their hideout."

Her story made perfect sense to him. "How long ago did they ride out?"

"Two days ago."

Lane nodded. "Were they all heading to the ranch?"

"I don't know for sure. I just know that they all rode out together that day."

His mood grew grim. Lane was familiar with the Circle D Ranch. It was a good distance away, probably close to a week's ride. Lane knew if he rode hard and fast, he might still be able to catch up with Cooper and his gang before they made it to the ranch and got settled in.

"Why are you telling me this? You know you're putting yourself in danger by helping me."

Dolly looked up at him, and as their gazes met, he could see fierce emotion blazing in her eyes.

"I hate Seth and Dan, and all those gunmen! They're nothing but animals—filthy, horrible animals—" Her fury was so great, her words were choked off.

"What did they do to you?" Lane heard the pain in her voice and knew there was more to the story.

"It wasn't what they did to me. It's what Seth did to my friend Francie," she answered, trying not to cry.

Lane tensed as he waited to hear what she was going to tell him.

"Seth beat her so badly . . . He broke her arm, and she's so bruised and battered . . . She can't work now. She can barely get around, she's in such pain . . . I wish I'd known what he was doing to her, but I didn't until it was all over and they were gone." Dolly angrily wiped away her tears. "Then when she couldn't work anymore, Harold threw her out."

"Where is she now?"

"Reverend Thompson and his wife have been helping her."

"So there are some good people in this town," he said solemnly.

"Yes, but they know just how evil—and deadly—Dan Cooper and his men can be. Most of them are too scared to do anything about the gang." Dolly looked up at him. "I want you to find them, Ranger Madison, and make them pay for all the horrible things they've done!"

Lane went to her and looked her straight in the eye as he told her, "I will."

The power of her emotions left her trembling as she whispered a heartfelt, "Thank you."

"Do you want me to walk you back to your room?" he offered, concerned for her safety.

"No! We can't be seen together. No one can ever know that I'm the one who told you about the gang." She stood up to leave.

"Don't worry. No one will ever find out from me. You have my word on it."

Dolly stared up at him in the lamplight, taking in the sight of him standing before her with his shirt off. He looked so handsome. He was a good man—a truly good man, and they were so hard to find in a town like Black Rock. She regretted that she hadn't been able to get him up to her room at the saloon, but she also knew he wasn't like any man she'd ever met before. "I have to go."

"Be careful."

"You, too." She started from the room.

"Dolly—"

She looked back at the Ranger.

"Thank you."

"Find them . . . ," she whispered as she left the room. She closed the door quietly behind her, leaving Lane alone.

Destiny had no idea how long she'd been standing over Bryce's inert body, trembling in horror. She was immobilized by terror, for she feared he was dead. He lay facedown on the floor, bloodied and unmoving.

Panic filled her, and she knew she had to run away. She knew she couldn't leave by the front door for fear that one of the servants might see her. She rushed to let herself out a pair of French doors that led to the balcony. It wasn't easy climbing over the railing in her dress, but she did it, and then clutching the torn bodice of her dress to her, she fled into the darkness of the night.

Destiny remembered Sylvia's earlier offer of help, and she knew the servant's home was one place she would be safe for the time being. She ran through the night-shrouded alleyways, trying to stay out of sight and praying Sylvia would be at her home where she lived with her thirteen-year-old daughter, Mary. Destiny's relief was great when she saw the soft glow of a lamp coming from the front window of the small cottage located behind her own house. Destiny ran up to knock quietly on the back door.

Sylvia heard the knock and went to see who in the world could be at her door at this time of the night.

She opened the door and was completely shocked to see Destiny standing there, her lip swollen and her gown torn.

"Come in—Hurry—" she whispered, urging Destiny inside as she looked up and down the alley to make sure no one else had seen her. She closed and locked the door behind her and then quickly pulled down the window shade to ensure no one would be able to look in. She turned to Destiny and saw the misery in her expression. Sylvia led her over to the small sofa so she could sit down.

"Who is it, Mother?" Mary asked, appearing in the doorway. She gasped at the sight of Destiny looking so abused and ran to her mother's side.

"Mary—go to your room—" Sylvia insisted.

"No, I want to help," the girl said.

Sylvia sat down beside Destiny, and Mary stayed nearby, looking on nervously. "Destiny—What happened? Who did this to you?"

Destiny was trembling as she told her friend the awful tale. "He was terrible . . . ," she managed, realizing for the first time that her lip was swollen where he'd slapped her.

"Who was?" Sylvia asked, expecting to hear that Raymond had attacked Destiny.

"Bryce Parker—It was Bryce—He tried to force himself on me, and when I resisted him, he hit me—" She went on to tell them all that had happened, how

Bryce had told her Raymond had sold her to him to pay off his debts.

"Mr. Howard is a horrible man. I knew it." Sylvia swallowed nervously as she asked, "Are you sure Bryce is dead?"

"I think so—He wasn't moving, and there was blood—" Destiny lifted her tortured gaze to Sylvia's. "Oh, Sylvia, I have no place to go—I can't go home ever again—"

"I know . . ." Sylvia had had enough. She had loved Destiny almost as if she were her own daughter, and there was no way she was going to let the girl suffer any more because of Raymond and his horrible ways.

"What am I going to do?" Destiny asked tearfully.

"I heard some talk a few days ago from one of my friends about a situation that might help us—"

"What kind of situation?"

"Let me check on it and see. You wait here with Mary. I'll be back shortly."

"Where are you going?"

"Don't worry about that. I'll explain once I know all the details."

"But Mother, what should I do if someone comes here?" Mary asked, truly frightened by everything that was happening.

"Go back in my bedroom with Destiny and stay there. Don't come out no matter what."

"All right."

Mary led Destiny back to the safety of her mother's room.

Sylvia slipped out of the house, locking the door behind her, and hurried off down the alleyway. She had to move fast if she was going to be able to save Destiny. She couldn't let anyone find the girl—not after what had just happened. Faithful servant that she'd been to Miss Annabelle, there was no way she was going to let Destiny come to any further harm. Somehow, someway, she was going to get her safely out of town that very night, and she had a pretty good idea of how she was going to do it.

Bryce stirred and slowly began to regain consciousness. He tried to sit up but groaned aloud as the movement sent violent pain shooting through his head and face. He collapsed back on the floor and lifted one hand to his throbbing forehead. He felt the wetness there and took his hand away to discover it was covered in blood. Rage filled him as he slowly began to recall what had happened.

"Destiny . . ." Bryce snarled her name as he finally managed to pull himself up to sit on the sofa. The pain was still savage, but his anger sustained him. He looked around, and when he saw the shattered remains of the vase on the floor, he realized what she'd done. "You little bitch—You're not going to get away with this . . ."

He struggled to his feet and staggered toward the door. As soon as he got himself cleaned up, he was going after her. He paused as he passed by a small mirror on the wall and was horrified by his own reflection. He realized then that he was cut up so badly he was going to have to send a servant for the doctor. Throwing the door wide, he slammed out into the hall, shouting for one of the servants as he moved unsteadily toward the staircase.

The sleepy-looking doorman appeared a moment later and was shocked at the sight of Bryce leaning weakly against the wall, covered in blood.

"Mr. Parker! What happened?" He rushed to put an arm around his employer to help support him.

"To hell with what happened!" he snapped. "Get me upstairs and send someone for the doctor!"

The servant said no more as he helped Bryce up the steps to his bedroom and onto the bed. He dampened a towel from the pitcher of water on his dressing table and gave it to Bryce before hurrying from the room to find someone to go for the doctor.

It was almost an hour later when Dr. Murray finished tending to Bryce's injuries. He'd had to wrap the injured man's head in bandages to stop the bleeding.

"You were very lucky, Bryce," the physician told him, his tone reflecting the seriousness of the injuries. "You will make a complete recovery, but you could have been killed. Who did this to you? You need to let the law know right away!"

Bryce glared up at the doctor from where he was sitting on the side of his bed. "You don't have to worry about getting the law involved. I'll handle this myself."

"But—"

"You heard me!"

"All right."

"And you don't need to mention this to anyone. Do you understand?"

"Yes." Doctor Murray knew what a powerful, influential man Bryce Parker was. He also knew the man had made some enemies over the years with his cut-throat business dealings. He assumed that it was those business dealings that had caused the confrontation he'd been involved in. He said no more about going to the law, but he advised his patient, "As it is—you are going to have scars, but you will be all right."

"Scars?" Bryce was suddenly concerned. He hadn't thought about the possibility of scarring. He'd always prided himself on his good looks. He shifted his position to look at his own reflection in the dresser mirror, and the image that stared back at him actually unnerved him a little. His head and face were mostly swathed in bandages. "How badly am I going to be scarred?"

Dr. Murray also knew what a vain man Bryce was,

but he didn't want to lie to him. That would only make things worse when the time came to take off the bandages. It was better to be forthright from the beginning. "The right side of your face had several deep cuts. There will definitely be some scarring there."

Bryce swore under his breath.

"The best thing for you right now is rest. Is there anything more I can do to help you?"

Bryce looked up at the doctor, all the hatred he was feeling in his hardened gaze. "No."

"I'll be back to check on you in a day or two, unless I hear from you." The doctor gathered up his supplies and prepared to leave.

Bryce said nothing more. He was just glad when the doctor was finally gone.

He sat on the bed staring at his own reflection in the mirror for a time, until a knock at his bedroom door interrupted his dark thoughts of how he was going to seek his revenge.

"Come in."

The maid opened the door to inquire, "Is there anything I can do for you, sir?" She tried to mask her reaction to the sight of him so heavily bandaged, but she couldn't hide it completely.

Bryce saw that she was frightened by him, and her fear infuriated him even more. He was used to charming women with his slick good looks, not scaring them. "Yes. There's something you can do for me—"

"What is it?"

"Bring me a bottle of whiskey."

"Yes, sir." She hastened to do as he'd bid.

As he sat alone in his bedroom drinking, Bryce made his plans. First thing in the morning he was going to find Destiny, and he was going to pay her back for what she'd done. If it hadn't hurt so much, Bryce would have smiled at the thought of how much he was going to enjoy his vengeance. He kept drinking until the liquor had numbed his pain enough so he could sleep. Morning couldn't come soon enough as far as he was concerned.

Chapter Six

Lane was saddled up and riding out at sunup. He had a lot of miles to cover to catch up with the gang.

Thanks to Dolly, though, he was hot on their trail. Without her help, it might have taken him another week or two to get the leads he needed to go after the gang. He smiled, impressed by the girl's bravery in seeking him out and grateful for the information she'd given him.

After Dolly had left the hotel, Lane had made a visit to the preacher's small home out behind the church. He'd met with the reverend and given him the money he'd won playing poker to help take care of the injured girl. When he'd taken his leave of Reverend Thompson a short time later, the reverend had agreed to send a telegram for Lane first thing in the morning.

It was just after eight when the telegraph office opened and Reverend Thompson showed up to send the wire requesting the Texas Rangers send additional men to the Circle D.

"Willy, I have an important telegram to send," the preacher told him as he handed over the message.

Willy read it quickly and looked up at the preacher nervously. "Are you sure you want to do this?"

"I'm sure." The man of God spoke with conviction.

Willy just shook his head as he got ready to send the wire. When he was finished, he looked up at the preacher.

"That's going to be one wild wedding—"

"What are you talking about?" Reverend Thompson asked.

"Before they rode out, one of the gang—I think his name was Seth—Seth Rawlins—Well, he went and ordered himself a mail-order bride to meet him in Bluff Springs. That's the town nearest the ranch Dan Cooper won in that poker game."

"But Seth Rawlins is an outlaw—"

"His mail-order bride ain't gonna find that out until it's too late."

The preacher was saddened by the news, but he knew a Ranger was on his way to straighten the whole mess out. For the woman's sake, he hoped Ranger Madison got to the Circle D in time. For an innocent woman to arrive in the midst of such turmoil would be terribly dangerous. He looked down at the telegraph operator seated before his instrument. Knowing Willy was a member of his congregation, he said,

"Keep the woman in your prayers, Willy. I have a feeling she's going to need all the help she can get."

"I'll do that, Reverend."

Reverend Thompson went on about his duties, but as he did, he said a prayer that both the Ranger and the young woman would be safe.

Raymond had been sleeping soundly after his wild night of celebrating when he was jarred from his sleep by a loud pounding on his bedroom door.

"What is it?" he called out in confusion.

"Sir, you're needed downstairs right away."

"Why?" he demanded grouchily.

"You have a visitor, sir," the maid responded. "Mr. Parker is here to see you, and he says it's urgent."

"Bryce is here?" Raymond grumbled, throwing himself out of bed.

"He's waiting for you in your study."

Raymond could only imagine that the other man had good news for him. After all, things had worked out perfectly for both of them the night before. Maybe Bryce had just shown up this morning to let him know that he and Destiny had eloped last night and were now happily married. If so, it would be the best news Raymond had gotten from anyone in a long time.

Raymond pulled on his clothes and hurried out of his room.

When Raymond walked into the study, he found out very quickly that the news Bryce had for him was not good—not good at all. The other man looked furious, and his head and face were heavily bandaged.

"Bryce! What happened to you?" Raymond asked, shocked. He quickly closed the door behind him to give them the privacy they needed to talk.

Bryce turned his icy glare on the other man. "Let's just say the evening didn't work out quite the way I had expected it to."

"I don't understand—Who hit you?"

"Your precious little stepdaughter, that's who!" Raymond raged. "And I want to see her *now*! Get her for me, or I'll go upstairs and drag her down here myself!"

Raymond rushed from the room and called the maid, ordering her to wake Destiny and bring her down to the study immediately.

Sylvia did as she was told and returned to the study only minutes later, looking most mortified.

"Mr. Howard, I have most distressing news. I expected to find Miss Destiny still in bed sleeping, but—"

"But what?" he demanded, turning on her threateningly.

She looked at him nervously. "Her bed hasn't been slept in all night! I searched everywhere in the house, but I couldn't find her. I don't know where she could be!"

Raymond rushed past the maid and up the stairs to Destiny's room. He found himself staring around the empty bedroom. He checked her closet to find all her clothes were there. Then he turned back to the maid, who'd followed him.

"When did you see her last?"

"Why, last evening," Sylvia replied. "When she was leaving the house with you to go to Mr. Parker's."

"Has anyone seen her since?"

"I don't know—I'll go check with the other servants," she assured him, playing her role as dutiful servant. She was relieved when Raymond didn't press her further. It wasn't often she was forced to lie, but this time she was going to make sure he never found out the truth. He was just as horrible and evil as Bryce Parker.

Raymond returned to the study to tell Bryce what he'd learned.

Bryce was not happy. He looked up at the other man, his eyes shining with hatred and the need for revenge. "I'm going to find your precious little stepdaughter, and when I do . . . she's going to pay!"

Raymond swallowed nervously and knew Destiny was in big trouble. He hardly felt sorry for her, though. He just hoped that Bryce's rage didn't come down on him in the end. This battle was, after all, between Bryce and Destiny. He'd held up his part of the bargain. It wasn't his fault Bryce couldn't convince her to marry him.

"I understand," Raymond told Bryce. "Where do you want to start looking for her?"

"We'll start with her friends—with anybody she might have confided in or gone to for help."

Raymond wanted to find out what had happened between Bryce and Destiny last night to cause her to run away from home, but he knew better than to ask. Clearly, Bryce had come out the loser in their confrontation. Knowing what a vengeful man Bryce could be, Raymond was sure Destiny was going to pay the price for having made an enemy out of him. Raymond had no idea what Bryce intended to do to her once he'd found her, and he didn't want to know. He would do what he could to help the other man track her down. He couldn't risk having Bryce call his debt back in.

Chapter Seven

Lane had managed to pick up the gang's trail just out of town, and for the next day and a half, he stayed after them as they headed for the Circle D Ranch. Based on what Dolly had told him, he'd assumed they would ride to the ranch together, and then Cooper and the other men would move on while Seth settled in and took over running the place. So Lane was surprised and troubled when on the afternoon of his second day of tracking them, their trails split up. One lone rider continued on toward the ranch while the rest of the gang headed north.

The discovery left him deeply troubled. Lane knew he was on the right trail. He knew he could follow Seth and easily catch up with the outlaw before he reached the ranch. Then he could wait at the ranch for the rest of the gang to show up. But he also knew he was only a day or so behind the main body of the gang. He was close to catching the killer Dan Cooper and the rest of his men, and if he could bring them in . . .

Lane stared off after Seth's trail for a long moment, trying to decide what to do. He wanted to arrest them all, but he couldn't be in two places at once. Since they had gone in different directions, Lane thought it likely that the gang might be getting ready to hold up another stage or rob another bank, which meant more innocent people might be killed.

That final realization made the decision for Lane, and he forgot about tracking down Seth.

Lane went after Dan Cooper and his gunmen.

It wouldn't be easy bringing down the four outlaws on his own, but Lane was confident he could find a way. Once he'd taken care of them, he would go after Seth Rawlins.

Lane followed the gang's trail until dark and then was up before dawn the next day, eager to close in on them. He was convinced that nothing was going to stop him from catching up with Cooper. Then, around mid-morning, he saw black, roiling storm clouds coming in from the northwest. The storm was going to be a bad one, and Lane grew angry. He urged his horse to an even faster pace, hoping he could spot the gang in the distance, but his luck had run out. The storm struck swiftly and savagely. The harsh, torrential rains lasted for several hours and scoured the land. When, at last, the rain stopped, Lane rode out again, but he could find no trace of the gang's trail.

Frustration filled him. He wanted to keep searching in hopes that he might find some clue to the direction they were headed, but after several hours, he gave up. There was only one thing left for him to do—he was going after Seth Rawlins, and he would be ready and waiting at the Circle D when Cooper and his men showed up.

Seth was feeling real good as he stretched out next to his small campfire and took a deep drink from the flask of whiskey he carried with him. After parting from Dan, he'd slowed his pace and had taken his time. He'd wanted to relax for a while and enjoy not having anything to do for a few days before showing up at the Circle D. Now, though, he was getting close, and after one more day of travel he'd be at 'his' ranch.

Seth couldn't help chuckling as he took another drink. Living the ranching life was going to be a lot different from what he was used to, but he wasn't sorry for the change. The law had been closing in on the gang lately, so he believed Dan had been right to come up with this plan. Everything was going to work out just fine as long as he made sure from the very beginning that his ranch hands knew not to cross their new boss. If any of them gave him any trouble, well, he'd make sure they paid the price.

Up until that night, Seth hadn't given much thought to the mail-order bride he'd sent for right before leaving Black Rock. Now as he lay alone in the night, he let himself consider that soon he was going to be a married man. He grinned at the thought. He wasn't sure just how long it would take the woman to show up, but he knew he was going to enjoy having a willing female around whenever he was in the mood. And not having to pay for his pleasure anymore was going to be mighty nice.

Seth's only concern was that his soon-to-be bride might be ugly. Even as he thought about it, though, he knew he could always turn out the lamp in the bedroom before he took her, and he could stay away from her during the day, working stock, so he wouldn't have to look at her. And even if she did turn out to be homely, her cooking had to be better than what he'd been living with these last years. All in all, he was actually looking forward to starting up his new life on the Circle D.

Again he chuckled, thinking of himself as a married man getting a home-cooked meal every night.

It was then that a deep, harsh voice resounded through the night.

"You're laughing, Rawlins. Do you think something's funny?"

Seth was shocked. He hadn't heard anyone ride up on him! He started to draw his gun, but a shot rang out, kicking up dirt right next to where he was lying. He froze.

"Try that again and you're a dead man," the voice stated coldly.

Seth was shaking as he stared into the darkness in the direction of the man's voice. As he watched, a man holding his gun on him stepped forward, and in the low light of the campfire, he could see the glint of the Texas Ranger's badge pinned on the stranger's shirt.

Lane kept his gun trained on the outlaw as he stared down at him. "Keep your hands where I can see them."

Seth knew he was in big trouble, and he knew he had to make a break for it. There was no way he could let this Ranger capture him. "What can I do for you, Ranger?"

"I'm taking you in, Rawlins."

"Like hell you are!" Seth erupted. In a frenzied move, he threw his whiskey flask at the Ranger, hoping to distract him so he could go for his gun.

Lane had known the man wouldn't give himself up easily. He had been expecting trouble, and he was ready when Rawlins threw the flask. Lane dodged it and dove for cover, returning fire just as Rawlins got off a shot. Lane watched as the gunman collapsed and lay unmoving on the ground beside the campfire.

Lane got up and approached warily. He kicked the outlaw's gun aside before turning him over to check his wound. He'd known the gunman wouldn't go down without a fight, but he'd hoped to take him alive so he could learn more about the gang's plans.

The fight hadn't played out that way, though.

His shot had proven true. Seth Rawlins wouldn't be riding with Dan Cooper's gang anymore.

It wasn't often Lane regretted being such a good shot, but tonight he did.

After burying Rawlins in an unmarked grave near the campsite, Lane took the time to go through the outlaw's gear. He'd hoped to find something that would give him a clue as to what Cooper's plans were, but he came up with nothing. The only thing he did find was a hefty stash of money. He didn't know where the cash had come from, but he knew it would help him with what he had to do next. The folks on the Circle D were expecting their new owner to show up, so he was going to take Seth's place and be ready and waiting for Cooper and his gang of killers when they rode in.

As dawn brightened the eastern sky, Lane took off his Ranger badge and hid it safely in his saddlebags. He was thankful now that no one on the ranch had met Seth before, and he hoped he would be able to make this work.

Lane put out the fire and then turned Seth's horse loose. He mounted up and rode out, hoping to make it to the ranch some time late that afternoon.

Lane's mood was tense as he faced the challenge that

awaited him. It wasn't going to be easy, pretending to be the other man while he waited for the day when the rest of the gunmen showed up, but, then, there wasn't much about being a Ranger that was easy.

At that thought, Lane managed a half-smile.

These next few weeks were going to be interesting.

That was for sure.

"Well, Rebecca, aren't you excited that we're finally on our way to Texas?" middle-aged spinster Gertrude McAllister asked Rebecca Lawrence, the young mail-order bride sitting beside her on the train during this first leg of their journey to Texas. She was Rebecca's official chaperone and escort to the town of Bluff Springs, Texas, where Rebecca's future husband, Seth Rawlins, was waiting.

"Oh, yes, ma'am. I'm very excited." Destiny smiled at the older woman.

Destiny hoped she sounded convincing, for 'excited' was hardly the word she would have used to describe the truth of her emotions at that moment. Fear filled her, but she couldn't let it show.

No one could know that she wasn't the mail-order bride Rebecca Lawrence.

No one could know that she had taken the place of the real Rebecca, an acquaintance of Sylvia's who had gotten cold feet the day before she was scheduled to travel to Texas to marry a complete stranger.

No one could know that she was running away from the terror that her real life had become.

So far, she'd managed to be convincing in her new role. She just hoped she could keep it up. She'd never thought of herself as an actress, but she knew her very survival depended upon it now.

"I'm sure this future husband of yours, this—" Gertrude quickly pulled the paperwork out of her small traveling bag and checked the man's name again. "This Seth Rawlins is going to be thrilled to see you. It's just a shame that it's going to take us so long to get to Bluff Springs. The next two weeks of travel are going to be hard, but I'm sure it will all be worth it once we get there. Why, you're going to be a rancher's wife when all is said and done."

"I know, and I'm going to have a lot to learn," Destiny said.

"You seem like a very smart young woman. You'll do just fine."

"I hope so."

"If you're brave enough to travel all this way to marry a man you've never met, I think learning how to live on a ranch will prove very simple for you." Gertrude understood why so many young women were going West to find husbands these days. She'd heard not too long ago that the men outnumbered the women twelve to one in a lot of the towns. It was no wonder some of the men sent back East for wives. A number of companies matching prospective grooms with mail-order brides had sprung up. The one Gertrude worked for even provided chaperones for the women traveling west.

"It will be different, that's for sure." Destiny looked out the window at the passing lush, green countryside and found herself wondering what the Texas landscape would look like.

"You'll be happy. Judging from the telegram your Seth sent, he seems like a hardworking man who's looking forward to marrying you and settling down. You'll have a good life together."

Destiny fell silent, wondering about her future. She had lost her mother and been betrayed by her stepfather. In St. Louis, she'd had Sylvia to help her, but now that she'd run away from the danger Raymond and Bryce presented, she was truly on her own.

Destiny told herself she could do this. She had taken on Rebecca Lawrence's identity as a mail-order bride in order to escape St. Louis. But she wouldn't jump from the frying pan into the fire. If her husband-to-be wasn't a decent, honorable man, she would refuse to marry him. She'd find some other way to make a new life for herself in Texas.

She just hoped her past never caught up with her.

The ranch hands at the Circle D had not been happy when they'd gotten the message from Chuck that he'd lost the ranch in a card game and that the new owner, Seth Rawlins, would be showing up soon to take over running the place. Chuck owed them back wages, and they were wondering if Rawlins was going to make good on their pay. A few of the men decided to just move on and had ridden out shortly after they'd learned what had happened, but most of the hands were loyal to the spread and had remained, hoping things would get better. They couldn't get too much worse. Chuck had not been the smartest rancher around, and he obviously wasn't a very good gambler, either.

Steve Barker, the foreman, was just coming out of the stable when he heard one of the other men call out that there was a rider coming in. Steve went out to meet the man to see what business he had at the ranch.

"Afternoon," Steve said as the tall, lean stranger reined in before him. "Welcome to the Circle D. What can I do for you?"

"My name's Rawlins," Lane replied as he swung down from the saddle and turned to speak with the tall, heavyset man. "Seth Rawlins. I'm the new owner of the Circle D."

"I suspected as much." Steve nodded to him.

"Heard of me, have you?" Lane asked with an easy grin.

"Chuck sent us word. It's good to meet you. Me

and the boys have been wondering how soon you'd show up. I'm Steve Barker, the foreman here on the Circle D."

They shook hands, sizing each other up.

Lane liked the way Steve looked him straight in the eye. He could see no deceit there and was glad. He needed to know he had reliable men around him that he could trust.

"How have things been going around here?" Lane asked, looking around at the ranch house and out buildings.

"We've had better times," Steve replied honestly. "Some of the men quit and rode out when we got word that Chuck had lost the ranch in a card game."

"Did Chuck owe you any back wages?" Lane had known there might be some difficulties taking over the Circle D, and he was ready to face them straight up.

"He did," the foreman answered.

"All right. Let me see what I can work out."

Steve was impressed that the new owner had even brought up the subject of wages. "How about I show you around?"

"Sounds good." Lane had realized as he'd ridden in that the Circle D had fallen on hard times. The house and out buildings were definitely in need of work.

Lane tied his horse up to the hitching rail and walked with the foreman down to the stable, where several of the other hands were standing around watching them.

"Boys, this is Seth Rawlins, our new boss. He's here, and he's ready to take over running things," Steve said, introducing him to the three men.

Lane shook hands with them.

"The rest of the hands are out working stock, but they should all be back in by tomorrow," Steve told him.

Lane spoke with the ranch hands for a while, wanting to learn all he could about the Circle D. His own years of ranching experience showed as they talked business, and the men were glad. They could tell right off that the new owner was a whole lot smarter than their previous boss had been.

Lane and Steve moved on to take a look at the rest of the buildings. When they passed the foreman's small house, Steve's wife, a pretty, dark-haired woman, came outside.

"Well, who've you got here today?" Caroline called out.

Steve took Lane over to meet her. "Caroline, this is the new owner of the Circle D, Seth Rawlins. Seth, this is my wife Caroline."

"Nice to meet you, Seth, and I do mean that," she said as she smiled up at him, liking what she was seeing. She thought the new man looked a whole lot sharper than Chuck. Caroline had never been one to mince words, so she just asked straight out, "I take it change is coming?"

Lane was struck by her forthrightness, and he was quick to answer. "For the better, ma'am."

"Good. Good. And please call me Caroline. All the other boys do."

"I'll do just that—Caroline," Lane replied with a smile.

She laughed good-naturedly. "It's good you're here, Seth. The Circle D needs you. There's some hard work that needs to be done around here, and Chuck never had the money. Can't say I'm surprised that he lost the ranch in a card game. I'm just real glad you're the one who won it."

"Well, I'm glad to be here," Lane answered truthfully. He hated to think what might have become of Caroline and the other good people on the ranch if the real Seth had shown up, intent on providing a hideout for a gang of killers.

"I'll be cooking your meals for you," she continued. "I'll bring 'em on up to the house if you like."

"Thanks. I know your cooking has got to be a whole lot better than mine," he told her.

"I don't get too many complaints from the boys," she said.

Lane and Steve headed to the main house then so

he could take a look around. It was a two-story structure with a full front porch that stirred memories for Lane of the house at the Bar M.

"Chuck didn't come back for anything, so you've got some furniture," Steve advised.

"That's good."

Lane followed Steve indoors, and they walked through the rooms. The house was sparsely furnished, but that didn't matter to Lane. He only needed a place to sleep. The main floor had a kitchen, dining room, sitting room and a small study, and there were two bedrooms upstairs.

"Chuck always kept the books there in the desk drawer," Steve explained when they went back outside again.

"I'll take a look at them right away. Thanks for showing me around."

Lane walked back to the hitching rail with Steve to get his saddlebags and gear.

"If you need anything, Seth, me and the boys will be down at the stable," the foreman offered.

"I appreciate your help."

"You're the boss," Steve said with a grin. "By the way, Caroline will have your dinner up here for you around five."

"I'll be looking forward to it."

Lane returned to the main house and stood just inside the front door for a moment, looking around.

He had been so focused on bringing down the Cooper Gang and making sure he could pull off playing the role of Seth Rawlins, he hadn't stopped to consider that he was going back to his old way of life.

He was going back to ranching. Lane forced away the painful memories that threatened and concentrated on settling in.

He had a job to do.

Dan Cooper could show up at any time.

He had to be ready.

Chapter Eight

Two Weeks Later
Bluff Springs

It was near noon when Destiny spotted some buildings in the distance as she gazed out the window of the stagecoach.

"Gertrude—That may be Bluff Springs!" she told her companion excitedly.

The older woman quickly looked in the direction she'd indicated and smiled. "Looks as if we're right on time, like Joe said."

When they'd started out early that morning, Joe, the stage driver, had told them that barring any unexpected trouble, he expected to reach town by midday.

Destiny said no more as the realization that they had finally reached Bluff Springs began to sink in. Soon, very soon, she was going to be face-to-face with the man named Seth Rawlins—the man who was to be her husband. She was a bit unnerved by the prospect, but with Raymond undoubtedly searching for her back in St. Louis, she had no choice.

There was no going back.

Destiny had come to accept her fate as best she could as they'd traveled over the long, endless miles of the untamed West. Thanks to Sylvia's quick thinking, she had a whole new identity and hope for a fresh start. Determined to make the best of her new life, she looked up to find Gertrude's gaze warm upon her.

"It's a little scary, isn't it, Rebecca?" the wise woman asked. She'd become quite fond of the young woman she'd been assigned to escort and had been impressed by her ladylike ways. The man Rebecca was going to marry was one lucky fellow—he was getting a beautiful young woman who was a true lady.

Destiny nodded, smiling slightly. "You could tell?"

"It will be all right," Gertrude reassured her. "You'll see. Judging by his telegram, your Seth sounds like an upstanding man. Just think, by this time tomorrow, you're going to be Mrs. Seth Rawlins. The wife of a successful rancher."

Destiny said nothing, but the thought of this unknown 'Seth' left her even more uneasy. If he was so successful, why did he have to send back East for a wife? She knew she'd be finding out all too soon.

The stagecoach kicked up a big cloud of dust as it came to a stop in front of the stage office in Bluff Springs.

"We're here," Destiny announced.

"Finally," Gertrude replied.

Their trip across country had been long and tedious at times. They'd had to deal with some awkward situations on the way. Heavy rains had washed out a road one day, and then the stagecoach had become stuck in the mire. When they'd gotten out of the stage to lighten the load, they had been attacked by hornets whose nest had been disturbed by their presence. That was one day Destiny would never forget. Then there had been the passengers who'd shared the close quarters of the stagecoach with them. Some had obviously never heard of the words 'soap and water,' and there had been a few screaming, crying children, too. Destiny and Gertrude had been the only passengers on this last leg of their journey, and for that they'd been grateful. Now, at last, they had arrived.

"Is Seth going to be in town to meet us?" Destiny asked. She tried to sound like an eager bride-to-be.

"No. According to what I understand, he's asked that you be brought out to him at his ranch. As soon as Joe unloads our bags, I'll look into finding a buggy and a driver who knows how to get to the Circle D." Gertrude was more than ready to take charge now that they had reached their destination. She would deliver the mail-order bride and stay long enough to witness their wedding before heading back home to St. Louis.

Their conversation was interrupted when Joe, the driver, threw wide the stagecoach door.

"Ladies, we are in Bluff Springs," he announced.

"You're a man of your word, Joe," Gertrude complimented him. "It's almost noon."

"I do try to stay on schedule. Here, let me help you down," he offered, reaching up to take Gertrude's hand.

She thanked him very primly as she climbed stiffly out of the stagecoach with his assistance. "It does feel good to get out and move around."

The driver turned back to help the pretty young lady who was traveling with the chaperone. "Here you go, Miss Lawrence."

"Thank you," Destiny said as she, too, exited the stage.

"Looks like there's no one here to meet you," he observed, a little concerned that two such fine ladies would be alone in a strange town.

"We didn't expect there would be," Gertrude told him.

"Do you need any help?" he offered.

"We do need to find our way to the Circle D Ranch."

"I'll tell you what. I'll go to the stable and see what I can find out for you. Just let me get your bags down first," Joe said.

"We'd surely appreciate it."

Joe swung the heavy bags off the roof of the coach.

"You stay right here," he directed. "I'll be back."

Joe left them safely there by the stage office while he went to check. True, it was daylight and a weekday, but in these wild towns, sometimes trouble happened no matter what time of day it was.

The stage driver's absence gave the women some time to examine their surroundings, and Destiny realized that life in Bluff Springs was very different from the existence she'd known in St. Louis.

"This town isn't very big, is it?" she said to Gertrude.

"You're not in St. Louis anymore, that's for sure," the chaperone replied sympathetically.

"One thing is certain—"

"What's that?"

"I don't think I'll be seeing any steamboats here," Destiny said with a grin, thinking of the St. Louis riverfront and all the boats on the levee.

They both laughed, knowing there was a big difference between Missouri rivers and Texas rivers.

"There is one thing I wish, though . . . ," Destiny said, looking down at her dust-covered, travel-worn clothing.

"What is it?"

"I wish there was time for me to get freshened up before we go out to the ranch to meet Seth."

"I understand your feelings. First impressions are important, but I'm sure that under the circumstances,

Seth will not expect perfect grooming. We've come a long way without the best of accommodations, and, honestly, even if we did take a room at the hotel to get cleaned up and change clothes, I'm sure we would be just as disheveled after the trip out to the ranch, especially if we end up riding out there in an open carriage."

Just as Gertrude was speaking, they heard the sound of a vehicle approaching and looked down the main street of town to see Joe riding up in a buggy that was being driven by another man.

"Ladies, this is Mick Baylor from down at the stable. He's agreed to take you out to the Circle D."

"Afternoon," called the wildly bearded, almost toothless Mick, giving them a big, warm smile.

"Hello, Mr. Baylor," Gertrude returned.

Mick guffawed. "I ain't no 'mister,' ma'am. I'm just Ol' Mick."

"Well, Ol' Mick, it's nice to meet you."

Mick smiled at the older woman and then looked down at her younger traveling companion. He gave the young one a good looking over, for she was real easy on the eyes. He couldn't help wondering what connection these two had with that new owner out at the Circle D.

Joe spoke up. "I'll load up your bags for you, and you can be on your way."

"We appreciate everything you've done for us, Joe,"

Gertrude said. Then she looked at the man named Mick. "I take it you know your way to the Circle D."

"Yep, I sure do," he responded as he got down to help the two women up into the buggy. "It ain't gonna be an easy ride, so you'd better hang on."

"How far is it?"

"Oh, 'bout half an hour or so. What business you got out there? You know the new owner? That Seth fella?"

"Yes, Miss Lawrence is his fiancée."

"Well, ain't he going to be glad to see you—" Mick grinned. Seth Rawlins had not only won a ranch in a card game, he had found himself one pretty girl. Mick wished he had some of the rancher's luck.

"We certainly hope so," Gertrude replied. This wasn't the first time she'd escorted a mail-order bride to her waiting husband, and she knew the first moments of meeting could be quite awkward and strained. She would have preferred to meet Seth in town in a more neutral setting.

"How far have you traveled?" Mick asked the younger woman.

"We're from St. Louis," Destiny answered politely.

"Welcome to Bluff Springs, missy. You're gonna like it here."

"I hope so." She smiled at him, sensing he truly meant his welcome. "I'm glad we've finally made it.

There were days when I thought the trip was never going to end."

"Let's get you out to the Circle D and deliver you to your intended." Mick slapped the reins on the team's backs, and they were off, covering the last miles of their journey.

As Destiny sat beside Gertrude on the hard, narrow seat, hanging on tightly as they headed for the ranch, she realized the moment had finally come. She knew from now on, she could never again think of herself as Destiny Sterling. She was Rebecca Lawrence, and soon she would be Mrs. Seth Rawlins.

Destiny offered up a silent prayer for the strength and guidance to get through what was about to happen. She prayed, too, that Seth Rawlins would be a man she could respect and enjoy living with.

Destiny knew little to nothing about the man she was about to meet and marry, but she knew Seth Rawlins was her future. She had to do everything she could to make this arrangement work out. Never in all her life had she imagined she would be a mail-order bride. She had always believed she would marry someone from St. Louis society, someone her parents would approve of and bless. She'd always imagined she would have a big, beautiful wedding.

The thought of her mother and father brought tears to her eyes, but she fought them back, struggling for control over her runaway emotions. It had been so hard losing her father; then she'd been heartbroken when her mother died too . . . She couldn't be weak now—or ever again. Her mother had raised her to be a strong woman, and, if ever there was a time in her life when she'd needed to be strong, this was it.

Destiny forced a smile on her face and stared out across the unending Texas countryside. It was wild and untamed, but it was also vast and beautiful. Gazing at the vast landscape, she made up her mind to find the beauty in her new life.

Lane was working in the stable with Steve when he saw a buggy in the distance heading their way.

"We've got some company coming," Lane remarked, frowning slightly. In the last couple of weeks, he'd been to town a few times and had spoken with some of the folks there, but he hadn't expected anyone to show up at the ranch for a visit.

Steve stopped what he was doing and went to take a look. "That's the buggy they keep down at the stable," he observed. "It's probably Ol' Mick driving. I wonder what he's up to?"

"I guess we're going to find out," Lane replied as he strode over to meet the approaching buggy.

Steve was too curious to keep working, so he followed Seth outside and went to stand with him as Ol' Mick reined in.

The sight of the two women in the buggy immediately set Lane to worrying. Seth Rawlins certainly hadn't had any family that he'd ever heard of, and he wondered if they were kin to the previous owner who'd lost the ranch in the card game. One way or the other, their presence might mean trouble.

If the women didn't know of the ranch's change in ownership, there could be an awkward scene. If they had any connection to Seth, his false identity was about to be revealed. He waited, his mood grim while he managed a welcoming, yet curious smile.

"Afternoon," he greeted them.

"Afternoon, Seth, Steve," Ol' Mick replied and then nodded toward the ladies. "I got a special delivery here for Seth!"

"I can see that." Lane smiled at the two women. "Hello, ladies."

Lane had no idea who they were, and he felt a surge of relief when he saw no sign of confusion in their expressions as they looked straight at him. He was thankful that they'd obviously never met the real Seth.

"They came in on the noon stage, and I wanted to get them out here to you right away," Ol' Mick went on.

"I appreciate it," Lane said.

"I take it you're Mr. Rawlins?" Gertrude inquired before descending from the buggy. She eyed the tall, dark-haired man up and down critically. She had to admit that with a bath, a shave and a haircut, he might be very handsome. It looked as though Rebecca was going to make out all right on this arranged marriage.

"I am," Lane replied, puzzled by her manner. It was almost as if she were inspecting him, looking for something, but he didn't see any mistrust or doubt in her expression.

Gertrude smiled brightly at him. "Well, it's good to meet you, Mr. Rawlins. I'm Gertrude McAllister from St. Louis, and this is Rebecca Lawrence, your mail-order bride."

Chapter Nine

Lane hadn't been sure what to expect, but it certainly wasn't this. He was unnerved by the announcement.

A mail-order bride?

What in the world would the outlaw want with a wife?

Lane didn't know how he did it, but he managed to keep the smile on his face as he dealt with the news. He stayed in control and calmly turned to the young woman who was sitting with Gertrude in the buggy.

"Miss Lawrence," he greeted the slightly nervous-looking blonde. "It's nice to finally meet you."

Destiny had watched the two cowboys come out of the stable as they'd driven up. She hadn't known if one of them was the man who, within a matter of hours, would be her husband, but she did now, and she was shocked.

Ever since they'd left St. Louis, she'd tried to imagine what a man who had to order a wife would look like. The image she'd come up with had, at times, been more than a little scary. She'd fully expected Seth Rawlins to be a desperate man, but as she gazed at the good-looking rancher standing before her, she knew she'd been wrong. There was nothing desperate about Seth Rawlins. He was tall and powerfully built and ruggedly handsome. Her surprise rendered her speechless for a moment.

"Hello, Mr. Rawlins," she finally managed in a rather timid voice.

Lane saw her look of perplexity and worried at it. He had no idea what information about himself the gunman had sent when requesting his bride; he was going to have to play his role carefully to make sure nothing went wrong. "Let me help you down."

Destiny stood as best she could in the tight space within the buggy. She turned to take his hand, planning to step down with his help, but Lane anticipated her action. He put his hands at her waist and lifted her with ease from the conveyance. Destiny braced her hands on his broad, powerful shoulders to balance herself and felt the hard-muscled strength of his body beneath her touch. When he set her before him, she looked up into his face, and it was then that their gazes met for the first time.

A shiver of sensual awareness trembled through Destiny as she stared up into his dark-eyed gaze, and the feeling left her even more unsettled. Embarrassed by her own reaction to him, she glanced away and quickly stepped back to put a more appropriate distance between them. She drew upon her mother's lessons to be a lady at all times.

Gertrude was watching them with carefully hidden amusement. She could tell right away they were going to make a handsome couple. She was about to speak up and ask the courteous rancher to help her down, too, when Ol' Mick grabbed her by the hand.

"Come on, little lady. I'll get you down over here," he said.

Before she could say a word, the driver had jumped out of the buggy on the opposite side and swung her down to the ground. Gertrude was more than a little disappointed. She'd been hoping Seth would help her down.

"Where do you want me to put your bags?" Ol' Mick asked.

Gertrude answered, looking toward the rancher, "I suppose that's up to Mr. Rawlins. Sir?"

Lane had to think quickly. He knew little about the way mail-order brides were handled, only that they expected to be married within a very short time of meeting up their intended. A deep pain filled him as he considered the choices he faced. After losing Katie, he'd sworn never to marry again, but now . . . "Why don't we take their bags up to the main house?"

Lane went to help Ol' Mick, and Steve stepped up to help, too.

"This is Steve, the foreman here on the Circle D," Lane said, quickly introducing them. "Steve, this is Miss Gertrude and Miss Rebecca."

"Howdy, ladies," he said, grabbing up some of their luggage. He looked over at his boss, smiling. "You never told us you had a bride on the way."

Lane was quick to reply, "A man's got to have some secrets in his life."

They were all laughing as they made their way up to the ranch house. Lane held the door for the others as they went inside.

Destiny stepped into the front hall with Gertrude and, unsure of where to go, they waited for the men to follow them in.

"Why don't you ladies have a seat in the parlor while we take your things on upstairs?" Lane directed.

Destiny and Gertrude took off their bonnets and set them aside on a small table in the hall before making their way into the sparsely furnished parlor. It was easy for them to tell that there hadn't been a woman's touch in this house for a long time—if ever. They sat down on the sofa to await the men's return.

"Well, my dear, you're here—You're at your new home," Gertrude said, patting her hand. Then she added in a whisper, "That Seth is one of the best-looking men I've seen in a long time. You're a very lucky girl."

"He is handsome," Destiny agreed.

"Very," Gertrude emphasized.

"What do we do now?"

"We'll discuss the wedding plans with him when he comes back down. We need to find out if there's a preacher close by who can marry the two of you tonight or tomorrow. I won't leave you until I'm certain you're legally man and wife. Are you excited?"

"I never dreamed it would be like this."

Destiny found she was being truthful with that statement. Never in all her wildest dreams had she thought she would travel to Texas and marry a complete stranger. She'd always fantasized about having a beautiful wedding. She'd fancied herself coming down the aisle in a white wedding gown and veil and having her parents in attendance. She'd always believed she would live happily ever after back in St. Louis.

Destiny knew now, though, those dreams were never to be. This was her reality. Her mother was dead and would never see her wedding day.

And then there was Raymond . . .

She had no doubt that her stepfather was still looking for her, and the law, too, after what had happened with Bryce. She was lucky she'd gotten out of town so quickly. There was no way of knowing what might have happened to her if Sylvia hadn't helped her to run away that night. Destiny didn't want to think about that. She forced the thought from her mind.

Texas was her life now.

Seth Rawlins was her future.

She was Rebecca Lawrence, soon to become Rebecca Rawlins, wife of the owner of the Circle D Ranch.

"Sometimes what life gives us is far better than anything we ever dreamed of," Gertrude advised.

Destiny didn't agree with that sentiment, but she said nothing as they heard the men returning.

"I'll go tell Caroline to plan on cooking up a big dinner tonight," Steve said as he let himself out of the house.

Ol' Mick came to stand in the parlor doorway with the rancher. "Is there anything else you ladies will be needing from me before I head on back to town?"

"I think we're just fine now. Thank you for bringing us out to the Circle D," Gertrude said. She got up and took several coins out of her purse to pay him.

Lane saw what she was about to do and quickly stopped her. "I'll take care of it."

The chaperone looked up at him with even more respect. "That's very kind of you, Mr. Rawlins."

Lane took charge. He paid Ol' Mick and saw him out. After closing the door behind the man, he started back to rejoin the ladies.

Lane paused for a moment there in the hall to ready himself for the conversation to come. He was about to deepen the lie that he'd begun when he arrived at the Circle D. He didn't like the thought of dragging an innocent woman into the danger he was facing from the Cooper Gang, but there was no way out of it right now. He had to maintain his cover. Everyone had to believe he was Seth Rawlins if his plan was going to work. Steadying himself for what was to come, he started into the sitting room to speak with the ladies.

Destiny was sitting on the sofa with Gertrude when he reappeared in the doorway. She felt his gaze upon her and looked up.

"The Circle D seems to be a wonderful ranch, Mr. Rawlins. You must be very proud of it," she said politely, hoping to start a conversation.

"I am, and, considering our circumstances, I think it will be perfectly all right if you stop calling me Mr. Rawlins, and start calling me Seth," he told her with an easy grin.

"All right—Seth—" she said, relaxing a little as she smiled back at him.

Lane had thought she was a pretty woman before, but now seeing her without her bonnet on, he decided she was downright lovely. He couldn't help wondering at the circumstances that had caused such a beauty to become a mail-order bride. He would have expected a lot of men to be pursuing her.

"That's better," he agreed as he seated himself in the chair opposite the sofa. He looked at the older woman who was sitting so properly before him. "I've never done this before, so I'm not quite sure what happens next."

"I think it would be most appropriate for the two of you to spend some time together. It's important that you get to know one another before the actual ceremony takes place. Is there a minister in town who could perform your wedding, say tonight or some time tomorrow?"

"Yes, there is," Lane answered as he hid his concern about taking such serious vows before a man of God while pretending to be Seth Rawlins. He told himself it wouldn't be a real marriage, that this was all just part of doing his job to bring down the outlaws, but still it troubled him.

"Well, good. Why don't I go freshen up a bit while you two visit?"

"You can take the bedroom on the right at the top of the stairs," Lane directed her.

Gertrude left the couple alone to get acquainted.

"Would you like me to show you around the ranch?"

"Please," Destiny replied. "I've lived in the city my whole life, so this is going to be a true adventure for me. I'm really excited about learning what it's like to live on a ranch."

He started to fill her in about his past as he led the way outside onto the porch. They stopped there to talk for a while.

"I haven't been here long. Less than a month actually."

"Really?" she asked, surprised.

"Yes, I won the ranch in a poker game."

"You did?" She was even more surprised by that news. "You must be an expert poker player."

He shrugged and grinned at her. "Sometimes a man has to take a chance, and sometimes Lady Luck is on his side. This time she was. I got real lucky."

"What was your winning hand?"

"A full house."

"What did you do before you won the ranch?"

Lane bent the truth as best he could. "I moved around, working at whatever jobs I could find, but I always liked ranching the best. That's why, when I won the Circle D, I knew it was time to settle down, and, since my luck was running good, I thought I'd take another chance and try to find a wife."

She decided to ask him outright. "Are you sorry you did?"

Lane was surprised by her forthrightness in addressing their circumstances. "No. Not at all. Having you here is proof that my luck is still holding."

"Thank you," she said softly, touched by his answer.

"What about you? Why did you agree to become a mail-order bride? Surely there must have been plenty of men back in St. Louis who wanted to marry you."

"My father died not too long ago. I know I'll always miss him. My mother remarried, but then she passed away less than a year ago, and I didn't have any family left. I'd heard how some women were becoming mail-order brides, traveling out West to get married, so I thought I'd do it, too."

"I'm sorry about your parents."

"So am I." She nodded. "I'm always going to miss them—especially my mother. We were very close."

"I know. It's hard losing a loved one."

"Do you have any family?"

"No."

She heard the slight edge in his voice and sensed he'd suffered a loss, too. "Have you lost someone close to you, too?"

"Yes."

"What happened?" She looked up at Seth, trying to read his expression.

Lane turned to gaze out across the land. "I was married once before, but my wife died."

Destiny was glad he was being honest with her from the start. "I'm sorry."

"So am I. Katie was a good woman." He turned back to her.

For a moment, Destiny could see the pain darkening his eyes, but then it was gone.

Lane went on to explain, "It's been a few years now

since she passed away, and after winning the Circle D, I thought it was time to try to settle down again."

Destiny couldn't help herself. She reached out to gently touch his arm. "Well, I'm glad you did."

He looked down at her hand on his arm and then lifted his gaze to her face, seeing only kindness there. The realization that Rebecca was a truly gentle woman made him uncomfortable about lying to her.

"So, tell me," Destiny asked, "what does it take to run a ranch the size of the Circle D?"

"A lot of hard work from sunup to sundown."

"How big is it?"

"It's over seven thousand acres," he told her.

"Seven thousand . . ." she repeated, impressed. The farms back home were measured in hundreds of acres, not thousands.

"It'll grow over the years."

"But isn't seven thousand acres big enough?"

He slanted her a sidelong grin. "This is Texas."

"Oh." She was suitably chastened.

"Come on, I'll show you around. We've been working hard, doing a lot of fixing up since I got here. The last owner had let the place run down a lot. When he lost it in the card game, he even owed the men back pay. I paid them what they were owed."

"You're a good and honest man, Seth."

Her words stabbed at him, but he didn't let his

unease show. "They're hardworking, reliable ranch hands, and they deserved what he owed them. I didn't want them to quit on me."

"It looks like you've done a good job around here. I was impressed when we rode in."

"Good. If we impressed you, then all our hard work is paying off."

They were laughing.

"Do you know how to ride?" Lane asked.

"I've ridden sidesaddle before," she said.

"That's a start."

He took her out toward the stable to look at the horses and to meet the ranch hands who were working on the Circle D.

Caroline had been outside hanging up some laundry on the line when she saw the couple leave the main house and start walking her way. Steve had told her the news about Seth's mail-order bride when he'd come to ask her to fix a big dinner that night, and now she went over to introduce herself. The thought of having another woman on the ranch delighted her. Sometimes she found herself feeling outnumbered by men. Having some regular female companionship was going to be wonderful.

"Seth, I understand you've got yourself a bride," Caroline said as she approached them.

"Yes, I do." He quickly introduced the two women.

Caroline sized the newcomer up quickly. Rebecca

obviously wasn't a timid or frightened young woman. She had to be brave to venture the journey west, and Caroline made up her mind to help Rebecca settle in and adjust to ranch life. "Welcome to the Circle D. You've got yourself a good man here in Seth."

"I know," Destiny replied without hesitation.

"I'm real glad you're here. It gets lonely sometimes, being the only female on the place."

"I'm glad you're here, too," Destiny said. She was going to need a friend to help her learn how to set up housekeeping in this rugged place.

"It's great to meet you, and I'll see you at dinner," Caroline said as she returned to her work.

Lane took Rebecca to the corral near the stable.

"Take a look at the horses and pick one out," he said.

Destiny studied the four horses in the corral. There was a roan, a pinto, a black horse and a palomino. She knew immediately which one she wanted. "I want the palomino. She's beautiful. What's her name?"

"Her name's Sunny."

Destiny smiled. "That name certainly suits her."

"Sunny's a very good choice for you. She's gentle. You won't have any trouble learning how to ride astride with her."

"Good. I don't think I'm quite ready to start trying to break in any horses just yet." She laughed at the thought.

"You will," he told her. "Just give yourself a few weeks."

"If you say so."

They were both smiling as they went into the stable to speak with the hands.

Chapter Ten

Gertrude had freshened up and then rested for a bit in the bedroom, awaiting Rebecca's return. The minute she heard her charge come back into the house and start up the steps, she went out to meet her in the upstairs hallway.

"Well? How did things go?" she asked, eager to learn how the couple was getting along. In the past, she'd heard stories of how some of the mail-order brides and would-be grooms had taken one look at each other and cancelled everything. Until the wedding vows had actually been exchanged between Seth and Rebecca, Gertrude was going to be a little apprehensive.

"It went very well," Destiny assured her. "Seth seems like a good man."

"I thought so, too. So, you're going to be happy with the arrangement?"

"Yes," Destiny answered without hesitation.

"Good. I'll go find him now and see about making the arrangements for the wedding."

"I believe he went into the study," Destiny offered. "I'm going to stay up here and get cleaned up. I want to wear a nicer gown for dinner tonight."

The long journey had taken its toll on her. She couldn't wait to get out of her traveling clothes and wash up. She was even hoping that that evening before bed she would be able to take her first bath in days. The crude accommodations along the stage route had provided little in the way of bathing facilities, so she was looking forward to soaking in a real bathtub.

"You do that. After all, this will be your first dinner in your new home with your fiancé."

Destiny remained there in the hallway for a moment, considering what the chaperone had just said—

Home . . .

She was home . . .

Tears burned in her eyes as she thought of her real home. The house where she'd grown up surrounded by the love of her doting parents—

She angrily pushed the thoughts away and reminded herself yet again that the woman she used to be—Destiny Sterling—didn't exist any more—only Rebecca Lawrence did.

And Rebecca would soon be Mrs. Seth Rawlins.

Destiny went into the bedroom where the men had left their bags and started to go through the few dresses Sylvia had provided for her to take along when she'd fled the city. Although she didn't have much in the way of a wardrobe, she wanted to look her best.

A short time later, Gertrude was waiting for Seth in the study while he went to send a message.

"Everything is set," Lane informed her as he returned. "I just sent one of the boys into town to ask the minister if he could perform the wedding tomorrow morning. Unless there's a problem and we hear otherwise tonight, Rebecca and I should be happily married by noon."

"Will the minister be coming here to the ranch, or will we be going into town for the ceremony?"

"That'll be up to him, but I imagine he'll want us to be married in the church."

"All right, in that case, I'll have my things packed and take them along with us when we go. That way, I can take a room at the hotel and stay there until it's time for me to leave for St. Louis again."

"You're more than welcome to stay here at the ranch," he offered.

"I don't want to risk missing the next stagecoach back, and besides, once you two are lawfully man and wife, Rebecca will no longer need a chaperone." Gertrude wanted to give the newlyweds the privacy they would need on their wedding night, but she hesitated to bring up such a delicate subject.

"I'll make the arrangements for you in the morning."

"Thank you, Seth. I'm glad everything is working out so well for the two of you."

"So am I. Rebecca is a lovely woman."

"Yes, she is," Gertrude agreed.

"Are you used to traveling alone?" He was concerned about her making the trip back East by herself.

"Oh, yes. I've done it before. Most folks don't bother old ladies," she said with a grin. "They know better."

He had relaxed a little in her presence, and at her comment, he chuckled.

Gertrude had always considered herself a good judge of character. In that moment, she believed she'd caught a glimpse of the real Seth and knew Rebecca was getting herself a good man.

"Rebecca is going to make you a fine bride, and I believe you're going to be a good husband to her," she said. "She's proven herself to be very capable on the trip out here. Not all Eastern ladies are so ready and willing to adapt to such a drastic change in lifestyle."

"Learning how to live on a ranch is going to be a challenge for her, but we talked about that when I showed her around the place. What about you?" Lane asked, teasing the chaperone a bit. "You could become a mail-order bride too and get yourself a husband. Then you could stay out here with us."

Gertrude knew he was joking with her, but she hastened to reply, leaving no doubt about her true feelings. "Oh, no—I prefer city living. It's more . . . civilized."

Lane thought privately that it was a good thing she was heading back East right away. If she thought life on the Circle D was uncivilized now, he could only imagine what she'd think if she happened to be around when Dan Cooper showed up.

"I've got some work I have to catch up on," he told her. "I'll be back here at the house in time for dinner."

"How soon will dinner be served?"

"Usually late in the afternoon. The foreman's wife, Caroline, will be bringing the food up here to the house, so until then, just make yourself at home."

"I'll do that, and we'll see you at dinner," Gertrude said.

Lane left the house and made his way to the stable. Knowing he had at least an hour before he had to worry about getting back to the house for dinner, he decided to take his horse out for a ride.

"Where you headed?" Steve asked.

"I've got a few things I want to check on. I'll be back shortly," he answered evasively. In truth, he just needed some time alone to come to grips with all that had happened that day.

Lane mounted up and rode out by himself. During his time on the Circle D, he'd found a quiet, mostly deserted place a few miles from the house. It was a shaded spot near a small pond. On occasion, he'd gone there to relax and let his guard down for a while, knowing for that short period of time he could be the man he really was.

Lane reached his favorite place and dismounted. He tied up his horse and then went to sit in the shade near the water's edge. In the peace of the moment, he took the time to look around at the quiet countryside. The years he'd spent with the Rangers had taught him how precious and fleeting these moments of peace and solitude could be, for at any moment, he knew, chaos could break loose—just like his mail-order bride showing up unannounced.

Lane found himself wondering, now, what he was going to do about Rebecca.

The following morning, they were to be married . . .

There was no way around it or out of it if he was going to keep up his pretense of being the real Seth Rawlins.

As a Ranger, Lane had always prided himself on being able to handle whatever came his way. He was always prepared for trouble, whether it was a shoot-out or tracking down criminals, but he had never even considered that he had to be prepared to accept and marry a mail-order bride.

He gave a weary shake of his head and almost wished he had a bottle of whiskey with him. But as tempting as the thought of a good stiff drink was, it would not clear his thoughts or help him figure out exactly what he should do.

Come tomorrow morning, Seth Rawlins would be marrying Miss Rebecca Lawrence.

The trouble was, he wasn't Seth Rawlins, and she was just an innocent young woman who was now caught up in a very dangerous situation.

Lane tried to find the bright side of the problem. He told himself he should be glad that he was the one running the Circle D and not the real Seth Rawlins. Rebecca would definitely have ended up in even more danger if the outlaw had been there to marry her instead of him, and she would have gotten trapped on the wrong side of the law.

Lane finally faced and accepted the truth about his dilemma—there was only one way he could handle it.

He had to go through with the wedding.

As he reluctantly accepted the hand fate had dealt him, memories of Katie that he'd long held at bay returned. A deep well of pain and sadness filled him as he remembered the joy of their wedding day all those years ago and the wonderful life they'd had together back at the Bar M. Their time together had been filled with love, and he regretted now that he hadn't lived each day fully appreciating the gift that their marriage had been.

Losing Katie had changed him.

It had hardened him.

He had sworn he would never love again.

The only emotion he allowed himself to feel any longer was anger. It was that emotion that had driven him to join the Texas Rangers. It was that emotion that drove him to track down murderers. And that was why he was there at the ranch right now. He was going to bring the Cooper Gang to justice.

He would do whatever it took to accomplish his mission, but he hadn't expected to find himself burdened with an innocent 'wife' who would only be in the way and cause trouble while he was trying to do his job.

Rebecca might be sweet and beautiful, but he wished he'd never laid eyes on her. The only thing that could save them both from becoming entangled in the lie of this false marriage would be the appearance of Dan Cooper and his gunmen that very night. But Lane knew that wasn't going to happen.

Drawing upon his inner fortitude, Lane vowed to himself that he would find a way to keep Rebecca out of harm's way while he brought down the gang. Once she found out the truth—

Well, they would deal with that when the time came.

Lane returned to his horse and mounted up to ride back to the ranch house, knowing he must remain constantly on the lookout for signs of the gang showing up.

He couldn't allow himself to be distracted by his new bride.

He could not let the gang take him by surprise.

He had to be ready.

Destiny had taken her time getting ready for dinner. She'd washed up as best she could and then had brushed out her hair and tied it back with a simple ribbon that matched the blue of the demure dress she was wearing. She knew her outfit was a far cry from the fashionable gowns she'd worn back in St. Louis, but those days were over. She felt she was lucky to possess the few garments she had. Fresh from a sponge bath, with her hair in a tumble of curls loose about her shoulders, she felt more like her old self as she went downstairs to help Caroline serve up the meal.

When Lane rode back in, he went straight up to the house. It was dinnertime. He was looking forward to Caroline's cooking, and he wasn't disappointed. The food the foreman's wife had prepared filled the house with a delicious aroma, and he eagerly started back to the kitchen. He'd just reached the doorway when he caught sight of Rebecca working alongside Caroline to dish out the food. He stopped, caught off guard by the change in her appearance. He'd known she was a pretty woman, but tonight, with her hair down around her shoulders and a simple blue dress that set off her blonde coloring to perfection, he found he couldn't look away.

"So you finally got back, did you?" Caroline remarked when she spotted him standing there watching them.

"I just rode in, and I'm glad I did. Dinner smells delicious."

"Well, you'd better get washed up if you plan on sitting at the table. We're just about ready to eat."

Lane hurried out to the pump and returned to join Steve, Gertrude and the two younger women for the meal of fried chicken, mashed potatoes and apple pie.

Destiny had known the food would be good just from the way it smelled, but she looked up at the foreman's wife and complimented her. "You are a wonderful cook."

"Why, thank you. I do enjoy fixing the meals. Have you done much cooking?"

Destiny reluctantly admitted, "No, I haven't, but I have a feeling I'm going to need to learn how to cook right away."

"That you will, with the husband you're going to have," Caroline teased, looking at Seth, who was helping himself to another serving of chicken. "He does have a good appetite."

"Would you have time to teach me?" Destiny asked.

"Of course, I'll be glad to."

"Good. Between learning how to cook and learning about the ranch, I think I'm going to be extremely busy for a while."

"Are you a fast learner?" Steve asked with a grin.

"I hope so."

They all laughed.

As they were finishing the apple pie, they heard a rider coming in, and Lane went out to see who it was. He was gone from the table for just a few minutes, and when he returned, he had the news they'd been waiting for.

"Everything has been arranged. Reverend Moore is expecting us at ten tomorrow morning," he announced, looking at Rebecca. "This time tomorrow night we'll be an old married couple."

Satisfied with the news, they finished off the meal with easy conversation and laughter.

"I'll spend the night out in the bunkhouse, so you ladies will have your privacy," Lane offered.

"That's very kind of you," Gertrude thanked him. "What time do we need to be ready to leave for town in the morning?"

"We should start out no later than nine o'clock to make sure we're there on time," he told her.

"We'll be ready," she assured him. "Won't we, Rebecca?"

Destiny looked up at the man who would soon be her husband. "Yes. We'll be ready."

It was after dark when Lane got ready to leave Rebecca and Gertrude alone at the main house. He walked out onto the front porch with his bride-to-be so they could enjoy a few minutes of privacy after the chaperone had disappeared upstairs. The night sky was starry, and the moon was just a sliver hanging low on the horizon.

"It's a beautiful night," Destiny remarked, gazing up at the sky.

"Yes, it is," he agreed. Then he said her name quietly, "Rebecca—"

She turned to look up at him questioningly.

"You're not having any regrets, are you?" Lane knew this was the last chance he had to find a way to call off the marriage. He still hoped to get her away from the ranch and out of danger.

Destiny smiled. "No. None. What about you?"

He gazed down at her there in the shadows of the night and couldn't help himself. Ever so gently, he drew her to him and answered her question with their first kiss.

The kiss was a soft, tender exchange, a far cry from

the brutality she'd suffered at Bryce's hands. To her surprise, Destiny found she was disappointed when he ended it and stepped back away, distancing himself from her.

"Go on inside," Lane directed. "I'll see you first thing in the morning."

She nodded and stepped back into the house.

Once she was inside, Lane made his way out to the bunkhouse.

Gertrude had already gone to bed in the extra bedroom, leaving Seth's room for Destiny to sleep in.

Destiny thought about taking a bath that night, but she was so tired, she decided to get up early and bathe in the morning. She wasted no time changing into her nightgown and getting ready for bed. She felt a little out of place as she climbed into Seth's bed, but once she realized how comfortable the bed was compared to what she had been sleeping on these past weeks, she relaxed.

Destiny's thoughts were still racing as she curled on her side and stared out the window at the stars twinkling in the night sky. She could smell Seth's faint scent in the blanket she had wrapped herself in, and she smiled, realizing for the first time in a long time, she felt safe and protected. Seth had been open and honest with her from the moment she'd arrived, and even tonight, he had given her the chance to call off the wedding if she'd wanted to. Though it pained her to admit she was lying to him about her name and her past, Destiny found she wanted to be there with Seth, and even more so after his kiss.

She closed her eyes and courted sleep, trying not to think about tomorrow night when Seth would be there in the bed beside her.

Chapter Eleven

Lane awoke just before dawn and lay in the top bunk, staring up at the ceiling, thinking about the day to come.

In just a few short hours, he was going to be married to Rebecca . . .

"You awake yet, Boss?" one of the hands called up to him.

"Yeah, Jake, I'm up."

"I figured you might be," Jake replied, chuckling from where he lay in the bunk below. "Hey, boys, don't you think the boss better get up and get moving?"

"That's right. He's got to go see the preacher man this morning. You even going to take a bath?" another added.

"I'm thinking about it," Lane remarked in good humor.

The men in the bunkhouse were laughing as they, too, began to stir.

Lane knew the hands were right. He was the

bridegroom, and he'd better look and act the part. He got down from the top bunk and pulled on his clothes and boots and started back up to the house. As early as it was, he believed the women wouldn't be stirring yet, so he could take his bath and get ready in the washroom off the kitchen. Lane quietly let himself into the house and set about preparing for the day to come.

Destiny awoke just as the eastern sky was beginning to brighten. She was nervous and, she had to admit, excited. This was her wedding day. It wasn't what she'd always dreamed of, but it was her wedding day nonetheless, and she wanted to look her very best.

She wasted no time getting out of bed and gathering up what she needed to bathe and wash her hair. Since it was still very early, she didn't want to awaken Gertrude yet, so she moved about quietly as she went downstairs to take her bath. She would wake Gertrude when she finished.

All was silent as she made her way to the kitchen. She was a bit surprised to find a low-burning lighted lamp on the kitchen table, but she thought that Caroline must have come up to the house for something a little earlier. Without thought, Destiny went to the washroom door and opened it.

Lane hadn't worried about heating up any water for his bath. He'd taken the time to shave and then had filled the tub with cold water and made short order of scrubbing himself clean. He had just stood up and grabbed his towel to start drying off when the door opened unexpectedly.

"What the—" he began as he looked up to find himself face-to-face with his intended.

"Oh, my—!" Destiny froze in the doorway, shocked by her first-ever glimpse of a naked man. She remained unmoving, staring at the magnificent specimen of manhood standing there before her. She took it all in—his broad-shouldered physique, his hard-muscled, tanned chest and powerful arms still shimmering with the glaze of water he had yet to dry off, his lean waist and . . . Heat burned her cheeks.

Lane was as shocked to see Rebecca as she was to see him. He actually found himself embarrassed to be standing before her so unclad, and he reacted quickly, strategically wrapping the towel around his waist to cover his more intimate body parts.

Lane had been cautioning himself ever since he'd come to the ranch that he had to be on guard every minute. He had warned himself that he had to constantly be on the lookout for trouble, but he'd never thought trouble would come in the form of this beautiful, innocent blonde walking in on him just as he finished his bath.

Seeing her distress, he said wryly, "Good morning."

"I—um—I didn't know you were in here . . ." Destiny began. Then, realizing how ridiculous she must look just standing there blushing, she forced her gaze to the floor.

"It's all right. I'll be done here in a minute."

"I'll just wait out here . . ."

She backed out of the doorway and made short order of closing the door behind her as she left. Once she'd closed it, she stood there in the kitchen, feeling quite mortified. She looked around in confusion. True, she had seen the lamp on the table, but she'd had no idea Lane had returned to the house, let alone that he was there in the washroom bathing. If she had known, she never would have walked in on him that way.

Destiny glanced back at the closed door and then had to smile slightly to herself as a vision of him standing there naked played in her mind. He was a handsome man, there was no denying that.

A part of her wanted to open the door again and get another look at the man who within hours would be her husband; she immediately scolded herself for her bold thoughts. She gathered her wits about her, remembering her mother's teachings on being a lady, and sat down primly at the kitchen table to await her turn to make use of the bathtub.

When Rebecca had backed out of the room and closed the door behind her, Lane had smiled and given a slow shake of his head. From the moment she'd showed up the previous day, she'd been taking him by surprise, and he had a feeling their time together as husband and wife was going to be just as unpredictable. The way he was feeling at that moment, he was beginning to wonder if he was up to it.

Lane quickly finished drying off and shrugged into his clothes. He didn't bother to button the shirt as he left the washroom to speak with her.

"Rebecca—"

Destiny had heard him open the door and thought she had enough control over herself to be able to speak with him. She turned to face him and was once again rewarded with the sight of his chest bared to her view.

"I'm sorry I walked in on you that way," she began.

"There's no need for you to apologize. You had no way of knowing I was going to come back up to the house this early. It was so quiet when I came in, I thought you were still in bed asleep." As he was speaking to her, Lane realized she was wearing only her gown and robe. Though she was completely covered from her neck to her ankles, he still found her enticing.

"I should have been, but I woke up early, and I couldn't get back to sleep—I guess I'm a little excited about today," she admitted. She felt his gaze upon her and became self-conscious over her own state of undress. She had never before had a conversation like this in her night clothes.

Lane gave her an easy smile, hoping to put her fears and unease to rest. "I'm glad."

"So am I."

"Let me get my things out of the washroom, and I'll heat up some water for your bath," he offered.

"Thank you."

As he set about helping her, Lane found himself wondering if the day was ever going to come when he would walk in on her while she was bathing. The image he conjured up of her was alluring, and he grew a bit irritated with himself. He knew he had to keep himself focused on his real reason for being on the Circle D, pretending to be Seth Rawlins, and the real reason he had to go through with this marriage—

Capturing Dan Cooper and his band of killers.

Bringing them to justice was the most important thing.

Lane brought in some fresh water to heat up on the stove, and then he emptied the bathtub to get it ready for her. After carrying the warm water into the washroom, he left Rebecca to her bath.

It was almost nine o'clock and time to leave for town as Destiny put the finishing touches on her hair. She had pinned it up in a fashionable, sophisticated style. She studied her reflection in the small mirror, and, even though her hair looked suitable, she had to admit this wasn't the way she'd always dreamed she'd look on her wedding day.

She had no white gown to wear.

She had no veil.

Even more upsetting was the knowledge that she wasn't surrounded by loved ones who were helping her prepare for the ceremony. There would be no wedding reception for friends and family afterward.

Destiny glanced down at the pale green, ordinary day gown she was wearing. It hardly qualified as the dress to be worn on the most important day of her life . . . But then she realized she was lucky to have even the few dresses she did own.

Destiny wished Sylvia could have been with her today to serve as her witness, but there was no way they could have traveled west together. It would have made it too easy for Raymond to track her down. Destiny had needed to get as far away from her past as she could and as quickly as she could. She had convinced herself that the past didn't exist anymore, and she hoped to make a new start away from the problems she's left behind. She never wanted to see Raymond again. He was an evil, cruel man.

As thoughts of her stepfather threatened, she could no longer deny the memory of that fateful night with Bryce. A shudder wracked her as she remembered his harsh treatment of her, the way he'd hurt her and tried to force himself upon her. She thought of Seth then and knew her future had to be brighter with him than it ever could have been with Bryce. Even though they had only known each other for a short period of time, she believed Seth was an honest man, and a gentle man. She hoped her first impressions of him were true.

Just then she heard a call from downstairs and knew it was time to leave for town. Destiny drew a deep breath and turned away from the mirror, ready to begin her new life.

Soon, very soon, she would be Mrs. Seth Rawlins.

Gracefully, Destiny left the bedroom to go downstairs. When she reached the top of the steps, she looked down to see Gertrude waiting for her with Seth in the front hall. They evidently heard her coming and looked up.

In that moment, Seth's gaze met hers, and she felt mesmerized by the sight of him. She still couldn't get the vision of him standing in the tub out of her head, but seeing him dressed as a gentleman for the first time set her heart racing. She managed a tentative smile as she started down to join them.

"You look lovely," Gertrude declared, coming forward to meet her at the bottom of the steps.

"Do you really think so?" she asked, still feeling a little unsure of herself.

"Yes," Lane declared, enchanted by the sight of her. True, she wasn't wearing a bridal gown, but with her hair done up in such a sophisticated style, she looked beautiful.

"Thank you."

Lane went forward to take her arm so he could escort her out to the carriage. "We've already loaded up Gertrude's bags, so if you're ready, we can leave for town now."

Destiny looked up at him. "I'm ready."

They went outside to find Steve, Caroline and some of the ranch hands waiting for them.

"Oh, Rebecca, you look so pretty," Caroline complimented her.

"Thank you."

"We'd better get going," Steve said as he stepped forward to help Gertrude into the carriage. "We don't want to keep the preacher waiting."

"I'm so glad you're coming with us," Destiny told Caroline.

"We were honored when Seth asked us to be your witnesses," she said as Steve gave her a hand up to sit beside Gertrude.

Lane made sure Rebecca was seated comfortably with the other two ladies before climbing up to sit on the driver's bench with Steve. He took up the reins, ready to make the trip into town.

"You know, Rebecca, you can still get out of this marriage. It's not too late!" Jake called out to her.

His remark drew good-natured laughs from the other men who were gathered around.

Destiny was laughing as she said, "But I don't

want out of this wedding. I'm marrying the right man."

"You are one lucky fella, Seth," another of the hands put in.

"I know," Lane replied, casting a quick look over his shoulder at Rebecca where she was seated behind him. "We'll see you boys later."

"We'll be watching for you! You know, you're going to be an old married couple just like Steve and Caroline when you get back here."

"I'm looking forward to it," Lane assured them.

The ranch hands were all chuckling as the boss started to drive away.

The trip into town went smoothly.

Destiny was still feeling a little nervous about what was to come, but as they neared Bluff Springs, she caught sight of the church steeple silhouetted against the sky, and she felt a sense of peace come over her. In that moment, somehow, she knew her prayers had been answered. Everything was going to be all right.

Reverend Moore had been watching for the wedding party, and he was ready and waiting to welcome them when the carriage pulled to a stop in front of the church.

"Good morning," the reverend said as they got down out of the carriage and came up the steps to meet him.

"Good morning, Reverend Moore," Steve returned,

and he made short work of introducing the preacher to Seth and Rebecca.

"So you're the new owner of the Circle D," Reverend Moore said as he shook hands with the rancher. "It's nice to finally get to meet you. Welcome."

They exchanged pleasantries for a few minutes.

Then the reverend looked at Seth and Rebecca. "I take it you two are ready to be married this morning?"

"Yes, we are, Reverend," Lane answered.

"Let's go inside," the preacher said, leading the way into the church.

They followed him in respectful silence.

Destiny looked around the small church, admiring the rainbow of colors pouring in through the sunlit stained glass windows. She found there was a deep, abiding sense of peace and grace there, and it soothed her even more.

With the preacher leading the way, they made their way in silence up the main aisle. Steve, Caroline and Gertrude took seats in the front pew as Reverend Moore drew the couple forward to stand before the altar. When he was certain they were ready, he began the ceremony.

"Dearly beloved, we are gathered here today to join this man and this woman in the holy state of matrimony . . ."

Chapter Twelve

"Do you, Seth Rawlins, take this woman, Rebecca Lawrence, to be your lawfully wedded wife, to have and to hold from this day forward, for better or worse, for richer or poorer, in sickness and in health, until death do you part?"

"I do," Lane vowed. The memory of the first time he'd made that promise played in his thoughts and in his heart as he repeated the words.

The reverend looked at the bride and asked, "Do you, Rebecca Lawrence, take this man, Seth Rawlins, to be your lawfully wedded husband, to have and to hold from this day forward, for better or worse, for richer or poorer, in sickness and in health, until death do you part?"

Destiny gazed up at Seth as she answered softly, "I do."

"Do you have a ring?" the reverend asked.

"No, I didn't have time."

He nodded and continued, "By the power vested

in me, I now pronounce you man and wife." He looked between the two of them, thinking they made a most handsome couple. "You may kiss your bride."

Lane drew Rebecca close and gave her a chaste kiss. He smiled down at her as they moved apart.

"Congratulations, Mr. and Mrs. Rawlins," Reverend Moore said.

As a mail-order bride chaperone, Gertrude had witnessed many weddings in her time, but she found there was something special about Seth and Rebecca. She hoped her feelings were right and that they truly did have a wonderful life together now that they were married. When Caroline and Steve got up to congratulate the newlyweds, Gertrude left the pew with them.

Lane spoke privately with the reverend for a moment, and then they all made their way from the church to stand outside.

Gertrude was feeling almost sad, for she knew they would now be parting company. She drew Rebecca aside for a moment. "You are a beautiful bride, and I hope you have a wonderful life with Seth."

"Oh, thank you, Gertrude." Destiny gave the older woman a warm, loving hug. "I'll never forget you—and our trip out here."

"It was an adventure, wasn't it?"

"Especially the hornets," Destiny agreed, and they both managed to laugh about their misadventure.

"I must be leaving you, Seth," Gertrude said, looking at the handsome groom, who was in conversation with the reverend. "I expect you'll take good care of my Rebecca."

"Yes, ma'am, I will," he promised, fully intending to do just that, "but don't leave us yet. There's one more thing I think you should see."

Gertrude was surprised. Most couples couldn't wait to get away from her once they'd married. She was actually honored that Seth should ask her to stay. "All right. What is it?"

"Reverend Moore just told me that there are some wedding rings down at the general store. Would you come along with us while we pick one out?"

"I'd love to."

They thanked the reverend again and then left to go to the general store.

Lane had been in the store only once before, but Steve and Caroline were well-known there.

"What can I do for you folks today?" Alan Hedgewick, the storekeeper, greeted them as they came in.

"It's very important," Caroline told him. "Seth and Rebecca were just married, and they need a wedding ring."

The balding, heavyset storekeeper happily congratulated them and then led the couple to a locked case near the back of the store. He unlocked it and took out a small box that contained several golden wedding bands. "Here's what I've got. Let's see if any of them fit you."

Lane picked up one of the smooth gold bands and looked at Rebecca. "What do you think about this one?"

"It will be perfect, if it fits," she told him shyly. Destiny was surprised to find that Seth wanted to buy her a ring. She looked up at him, her uncertainty evident in her expression. "Can you afford this?"

Lane saw the pure innocence in her eyes and knew her question was heartfelt. "Yes, I can afford it."

Without saying another word, he took her hand and slipped the gold band on her ring finger. It went on easily.

"It's perfect," Destiny said softly as she stared down at the ring on her hand.

The chaperone was standing nearby and was quick to agree. "Yes. It is. Now you truly are man and wife."

Lane couldn't help himself. He bent to Rebecca and gave her a chaste kiss right there in front of everyone. "Now, you're not done yet."

"What do you mean?"

"Caroline—" Lane looked at the foreman's wife. "I need your help now."

"What can I do?" she offered.

"I need you to help Rebecca pick out the things that she's going to need for living on a ranch."

"You mean you want us to go shopping?" Caroline

was surprised. She'd expected Seth to be like most of the men she knew. She thought he'd be in a big hurry to get back home after the wedding.

"That's right." He smiled at his bride. "We probably won't be back in town for a while, so go ahead and get what you need."

Destiny was caught totally by surprise at his generosity. "Seth—I can make do with what I've got. There's no need for you to spend your money on me—"

He stopped her quickly. "There's every need. We're married now. It's *our* money."

After her mother had died, Raymond had kept tight control over every cent of the Sterling family's money and had allowed Destiny very little in the way of funds. "Thank you."

"Come on, Boss," Steve said, grinning. "I think since you're giving the women free rein here at the store, we've got time to go over to the saloon and have us a little celebration over your wedding."

Lane directed the storeowner, "Put whatever they pick out on my bill." Then he smiled at Rebecca. "We'll be back."

Lane left the store with Steve. They both knew better than to stay around when women went shopping.

Gertrude was even more impressed than Destiny by Seth's generosity and told the new bride, "You certainly got yourself one fine man."

Destiny paused to watch the two men through the store window as they crossed the street and headed toward the saloon. "Yes, I do."

"Are you ready?" Caroline asked excitedly.

"Let's shop," Destiny agreed.

Lane and Steve entered the bar, more than ready for a drink. It was still before noon, so fortunately the saloon wasn't crowded yet. They went to stand at the bar and both ordered whiskeys.

The two saloon girls who were working saw them come in, but they didn't bother to approach them. It was well-known among the saloon girls that Steve was faithful to his wife, and they'd heard the rumor started by Ol' Mick that the new owner of the Circle D was all set to marry his mail-order bride who'd just arrived in town yesterday.

"Here's to your marriage," Steve toasted, lifting his glass of whiskey to Seth.

"Thanks."

They both took a deep drink.

"We might as well find ourselves a table and relax for a while," Steve suggested. Knowing his wife as he did, he figured they were going to be waiting in the saloon for a spell.

It was almost an hour later, and Destiny, Caroline and Gertrude were just finishing up their shopping.

Back home when she'd been much younger, Destiny had never been too excited about learning how to sew, but her mother had insisted she take lessons. Now that she was going to be living on the ranch, she realized it was a good thing that she had done so. With Caroline's help, she had gone through the dry goods and picked out some material that she could use to make practical, everyday clothing for herself.

"You're going to need some boots, too," Caroline advised, knowing the shoes that Rebecca had worn in the city were hardly up to ranch life.

They found a pair that fit her just as Gertrude approached.

"There's one other thing you need, young lady . . ." The older woman took her hand and drew her to the section of the store where ready-made clothing was displayed.

Destiny was hoping Gertrude had found a split riding skirt for her, but she was in for a surprise.

"Here—For your wedding night—" Gertrude picked up the carefully folded silken nightgown she'd found among the garments. "This will be perfect, don't you think?"

"Oh—it's lovely," Destiny said, surprised to find such a garment in the store.

"Good. I'm glad you like it. It's my wedding present to you," the older woman offered.

Destiny gave her a quick hug, touched by her thoughtfulness.

Caroline was smiling in approval. "Seems to me that's more of a present for Seth."

They all laughed.

"He'll be one happy man tonight," Caroline said.

Destiny blushed at her new friend's observation, and she was a little embarrassed as Gertrude carried the nightgown up to the front to pay for it. She'd never owned anything like the gown before, and she wasn't quite sure what the store owner would think when Gertrude bought it for her. Her concerns about the store owner were quickly relieved, though, when she discovered his wife had taken over for him and would be the one ringing up their purchases. She didn't even blink an eye at the lovely nightgown, and it wasn't long before Destiny, Caroline and Gertrude were leaving the store with their many packages.

"I'll go get Steve and Seth," Caroline said after they'd stowed their purchases in the carriage. "You wait here."

When she'd moved off, Gertrude was left alone with Rebecca. She gave the younger woman a hug. "I truly am going to miss you. Not all the young ladies I accompany are as dear as you are."

"I'm going to miss you, too, Gertrude. Are you sure you want to go back? You could stay here."

"No, my home is in St. Louis. I'm needed back there, but I want you to be happy."

"I will be, and thank you for everything—"

Gertrude had a twinkle in her eyes as she said, "Enjoy that wedding present I gave you."

Caroline made short order of calling Steve and Seth out of the saloon and soon returned to the carriage with the two men.

Then they all accompanied Gertrude to the hotel and made the arrangements for her return trip to St. Louis before saying their final good-byes. It was a tearful moment for Destiny. She had appreciated Gertrude's wisdom and insight during their time together.

When they left her, they went back to the carriage.

"Are you ready to go home?" Lane asked Rebecca.

"Oh, yes—"

Steve took a look at all the packages in the carriage and laughed. "It's a good thing we didn't bring the buckboard. They might have bought even more."

Caroline was laughing, too. "If I'd known Seth was going to let us go shopping, we would have done just that!"

Lane started to climb up and sit with Steve again on the driver's bench, but Caroline stopped him.

"Oh, no. You're the groom. You need to ride with Rebecca. I'll sit up there with Steve."

Lane didn't hesitate. He took the seat next to Rebecca and put his arm around her as they started the trip back to the ranch.

Caroline had secretly arranged for the ranch hands to have dinner ready when they returned so they could all celebrate together. As they drew near the house, they could see that tables had been set up behind the main house, so everyone could eat outside. When the ranch hands saw them driving in, they came out to congratulate the newlyweds.

Caroline went to help the bunkhouse cook serve up the simple yet filling meal he had prepared. Everyone ate heartily, and the time passed quickly as the men regaled Rebecca with stories about life on the Circle D. She enjoyed hearing their tales, and she didn't doubt one day she'd have stories of her own to tell about her life there.

The tables had been cleared, and someone had taken out a guitar and was softly strumming. As the sun started to set, they all knew it was time to call it a day and give the newlywed couple their time alone.

"Come on, Boss!" Jake urged. "Let's see you carry your bride over the threshold!"

Lane had been looking for an opportunity to take Rebecca in his arms, and now he had it. "You're right. I think it's time."

He took her hand and drew her up from where she'd been sitting at the table with him. Before she could say a word, he swept her up into his arms.

Destiny had known all day that this moment was coming, but even so, her heartbeat quickened at the realization that this was their wedding night. She linked her arms around his neck as he started up to the house.

Lane held her close as he went up the porch steps and shouldered the door open. He carried her inside, and then he carefully set her on her feet before closing the door to ensure their privacy.

"There's been something I've been wanting to do for quite a while now . . ." he told her as he lifted one hand to caress her cheek.

"What's that?"

Lane didn't bother to answer.

He just showed her.

He took her in his arms and kissed her.

Chapter Thirteen

The embrace started off as an innocent exchange, but before long Lane deepened the kiss and crushed her to him.

Destiny had been kissed by a few of her suitors, and she had suffered through Bryce's harsh embrace, but nothing she'd ever experienced before had prepared her for the excitement of Seth's passionate kiss. Being in his arms was ecstasy for her. She felt loved and protected.

"You are a mighty tempting woman," Lane said as he ended the kiss and looked down at her.

Destiny felt almost bereft that he'd broken off the kiss. "Why did you stop?"

Lane smiled at her display of innocence. "Because, my dear wife, if I hadn't let you go right then, I wouldn't be able to let you go at all."

She reached up and drew him down to her, whispering against his lips just before she kissed him, "Good . . ."

Lane let out a low groan at the temptation she was offering and gave up all his intentions of staying in control. Without another word, he lifted her into his arms again and quickly carried her up the stairs to the bedroom. He strode across the room to lay her on the bed, then followed her down, seeking her lips in kiss after passionate kiss.

Destiny had never lain in bed with a man before, but that was only a fleeting thought as she opened herself fully to Seth. Having the hard male warmth of him so close left her only wanting to know more as he slowly began to caress her.

"Oh, Seth . . ." she breathed, trembling a little at his bold touch.

"Easy, love," he murmured as he traced a trail of heated kisses down her throat and neck.

Destiny felt a stirring deep within the womanly heart of her and found herself arching against him.

She wanted more—

She needed more—

But innocent that she was, she had no idea what it was she wanted and needed from him.

Lane, however, knew just what to do. He sat up long enough to shed his shirt. He wanted a lot less clothing between the two of them.

Destiny's gaze caressed him, tracing over his hard-muscled chest. She had longed to touch him that morning when she'd seen him in the bath, and now there was no reason not to. She lifted her arms to draw him back down to her, her hands moving over the width of his broad shoulders and back.

Lane kissed her hungrily, and when she responded without reserve, he was encouraged and more than ready to make her his own. Her dress buttoned in the front, and he began to work at the buttons, wanting to strip away the garment that kept him separated from her.

Destiny found herself trembling as he unbuttoned her dress to the waist and pushed it from her shoulders. She knew a moment of shyness, but then he kissed her again, and she was lost.

With utmost care, Lane pushed the straps of her chemise down, baring her breasts to his gaze and touch. Destiny arched in unexpected excitement at the first touch of his lips upon her bared flesh, and all was lost as they came together in a blaze of desire. Caught up in the heat of their need, they stripped away the rest of their clothing and came together, as one, for the first time.

Lane was immediately aware that she had given him the gift of her innocence. He moved slowly at first, wanting to bring her pleasure in this, their first loving, but she was a firebrand in his arms, and he was soon lost in the heat of his driving passion. Destiny clung to him, thrilling at his touch, and ecstasy was theirs. They collapsed, wrapped in each other's arms, treasuring the beauty of what they'd just shared.

It was some time later that Lane raised himself up on one elbow and bent to kiss her softly. "You're beautiful."

Destiny gave him a very sensuous smile in return as she purred, reaching out to touch his chest. "So are you . . ."

She had known little about lovemaking before this night, and she was thrilled now that she had escaped the horror of Bryce's embrace for the haven of Seth's. With her husband she had truly found peace and love. When she had run away from her home, taking the chance of becoming Rebecca the mail-order bride, she had never dreamed she would be so blessed as to end up married to a man like him.

Wonderingly, she ran her hand over his hard chest. Her bold caress ignited the fire of his need, and Lane claimed her again, making her his own.

It was later that night as Destiny lay in the circle of his arms that she remembered the gift Gertrude had given her. She smiled in the darkness, knowing she would save the silken nightgown for another night. She certainly hadn't needed it tonight.

Raymond was beyond fury as he sat at his desk in the study, drinking heavily. His frustration at being unable to find Destiny had rendered him absolutely livid. It had been two weeks now—two weeks of unending searches that had turned up nothing, and with each passing day, Bryce was putting more and more pressure on him to pay back the money he owed or deliver Destiny to him. He knew Bryce had been searching for her, too, and it amazed him that with the resources they'd both used, they hadn't been able to find any clues to her whereabouts.

To make matters even worse, late that afternoon he'd been paid an unexpected visit by Marshall Westlake, the attorney who'd drawn up his dead wife's first will. The lawyer had heard the talk of how Destiny had mysteriously left town, and he'd come to check on her. Raymond had told him that he had no reason to be concerned. He explained that he and Annabelle had set up a new will and everything was fine, but the lawyer hadn't seemed to believe him. Westlake had told him that he was going to look into the issue of the new will the following day.

Raymond drained every drop of liquor from his glass as he worried about what the lawyer might do. He lifted his gaze to the portrait of Destiny and her mother that hung on the wall.

They looked so pretty and happy—and rich.

Raymond lost what little control he had.

"You bitch! Where are you? Where have you gone?" he raged. Unable to contain himself any longer, he threw his crystal tumbler at the portrait. He watched in drunken disgust as the tumbler crashed into the picture and shattered into pieces.

In a violent move, Raymond stood up and shoved his chair back against the wall. He stalked across the study to stare out the window at the street below. Within the next few days, Bryce would be paying him a visit, and he had to have some answers for him. If he didn't . . .

Raymond didn't even want to think about what was going to happen if he couldn't make good on the money he owed the ruthless businessman.

Again he started swearing, cursing. His plan had been so well thought out, or so he'd believed. He'd known about the will Annabelle had drawn up some years before leaving all her money to Destiny. He had asked her repeatedly over those last months to revise the will. He'd even gone so far as to retain a different lawyer and draw up a new will giving him control over his wife's money while promising to provide for Destiny's well-being, but Annabelle had refused to sign it. She had told him it was Sterling money and it would stay in the Sterling family. He hadn't argued with her at that point. He was enjoying his newfound access to the 'Sterling money' too much to cause a ruckus.

But everything had changed so quickly. Annabelle had suddenly gotten sick, and scared of losing his income and comfortable way of life, he'd taken matters into his own hands. He'd forged her name on the new will, thereby guaranteeing that his opulent lifestyle would continue and he'd have the full inheritance in his name.

But now her attorney was meddling and seemed to be on to him, and Raymond feared his plan might fall apart completely . . .

Raymond refused to blame himself for the current state of his financial affairs. True, he'd lost too much gambling. The mistake he'd made had been gambling with a powerful, dangerous man like Bryce. Raymond was angry with Bryce. The other man had agreed to take Destiny in settlement of the debt. It wasn't his fault Bryce had ruined the arrangement by scaring her off.

Raymond turned away from the window, lost in thought. Bryce claimed Raymond still owed him, and since Destiny had run away, he had been paying off the debt in regular small amounts. He knew if he tried to pay all of what he owed to Bryce in one lump sum, he would draw even more scrutiny of his monetary affairs, and he couldn't risk attracting such attention.

At that moment, a knock came at the door.

"What is it?" he demanded angrily.

"Sir, I thought I heard something breaking, and I wondered if I should come in to clean up?"

Raymond paused, his mind racing as he thought about the maid. He'd questioned her numerous times in the weeks since Destiny's disappearance, but she'd always told him she knew nothing about his stepdaughter's whereabouts.

"Come in, Sylvia," he bade.

Sylvia opened the door to see the shattered tumbler on the floor and knew her employer was in one of his drunken rages. "Oh, I'll get a rag and be right back."

"Wait one minute," he ordered. "I wanted to ask you—"

"Yes, sir?" she asked tentatively.

"It's been two weeks now, and I haven't heard a word from Destiny. I am terribly concerned about her well-being. Have you heard anything, anything at all, that might help me find her, or, at least, that would let me know she is safe?"

The maid looked up at him. She kept her expression carefully guarded as she answered, "No, sir. I haven't heard from her since that last day she was here. I don't know where she could be. I'm worried about her, too. I've asked around, but no one has seen her in town. At first, I thought she might have eloped, but there weren't any suitors she was seeing seriously. I'm afraid it's a bad sign that there's been no word from her—It's almost as if she's vanished."

"I know. I'm so afraid she's been harmed in some

way—" He tried to play the role of concerned stepfather. "But surely we would have heard something if that had happened."

Sylvia tensed at his words, and she actually wanted to slap him for being such a liar. She despised the man with every fiber of her being and had thought about quitting many times since Destiny had fled. She'd stayed on her job, though, for she'd feared that if she had tried to quit, Raymond might have figured out that she'd had a hand in helping Destiny escape.

"Yes, sir. Let me get the rag so I can clean up that spill for you." She hurried away. She never liked to be in close quarters with the man.

Raymond's anger still burned within him, and as he glared out the window at the darkness of the night, he found himself wondering just where Destiny was at that moment. He knew it was a good thing she wasn't right here with him, for if she had been, he would have beaten her within an inch of her life for causing him so much trouble. He stormed over to the liquor cabinet and poured himself another glass of the potent liquor.

Sylvia returned to clean up the broken glass and then let him know that she was leaving for the night.

Raymond said little as he watched her leave.

He just kept drinking.

It was over an hour later that the drunken Raymond

decided to go find the maid and question her again about the night Destiny had vanished. He made his way unsteadily from the main house and down the walk that led to the servant's cottage. Reaching the front door, he banged on it loudly, thinking since it was dark inside, she'd already retired for the night.

Sylvia was in bed when she heard the loud knocking at her door, and she had a dreadful feeling she knew who was there. She knew she couldn't just ignore the knocking and hope that Raymond would go away. He wasn't like that. Not wanting to awaken her daughter, she got up and threw on her robe and quietly closed the door to Mary's room, hoping the child would sleep through the disturbance.

"I'm coming," she called out quietly.

After lighting the lamp on the kitchen table, she hurried over to peer out the window. She wasn't wrong. Just as she'd suspected, the drunken fool was standing on her threshold.

For a moment, Sylvia was unsure what to think. Why was Raymond there? Had he learned something about Destiny? That was the only reason she could imagine he would have for coming to her home at this time of the night.

"What is it? Has there been news of Destiny?" Sylvia asked as she opened the door to him.

"I want to talk to you," he said drunkenly, walking past her and on into her small house without invitation.

"Raymond—You really shouldn't be here. It's much too late. I'm sure whatever you have to say could wait until tomorrow morning." She tried to convince him to leave, but it was pointless.

"Don't tell me what to do!" he ground out. "You work for me, and you'll do whatever I tell you to do!"

Sylvia knew then she was in real trouble. His temper had only gotten worse since she'd left him. "What do you want?" she demanded, hoping to get this visit over in a hurry. She wanted him out of her house.

He took a menacing step toward her. "I'll tell you what I want! I want you to tell me what you know—Everything, and I do mean everything!"

"I don't know what you're talking about," she denied.

He loomed over her. "Stop playing me for a fool, woman! With her mother dead, you're the only one Destiny would have gone to for help that night she disappeared. I've put up with your lies for weeks, but I'm sure you know more than you've been telling me, and I want the truth from you—now!"

Sylvia felt intimidated by him, but she kept her composure. "Raymond, I don't know where Destiny is. I've told you that before. Now, I want you to leave and go sober up—"

Raymond had had all he could take. He wasn't about to let a servant talk to him that way. Without thinking about his actions, he slapped her hard in the face, knocking her backward. "I want answers!"

He advanced on her, ready to hit her again. He backhanded her violently, bloodying her lip this time.

"Get out!" she cried, scrambling to get away from him.

But Raymond was too drunk to worry about the consequences of his actions. He closed in on her again. "Tell me what you know!"

"Don't, Raymond! Leave me alone!" She cowered before him as he drew near.

"I'm not leaving until I know where Destiny is!"

"But I have no idea where she is!" Sylvia protested.

Her answer only drew more of his ire, and he struck her even more forcefully, knocking her to the floor.

Young Mary had been asleep in her bedroom, but at the sound of the violence, she rushed from her room to help her mother.

"What are you doing?" the young girl demanded of Raymond, nearly hysterical at the sight of him beating her mother.

Raymond turned on the young girl, and in that instant, he knew he had the perfect opportunity to force the maid to talk.

"Well, well, well, Sylvia," he murmured. "If you won't tell me, maybe your daughter will."

"You leave her alone! Mary, get out of here! Run! Now!"

Even as drunk as he was, Raymond could still move quickly, and he blocked the girl's access to the door. "Oh, no, my dear. You're not going anywhere, and neither is your mother—not until you tell me what you know about Destiny's disappearance."

"We don't know anything!" Sylvia insisted.

This time he closed in on her, ready to use his fist, and the threat of even worse violence caused the young girl to cry out.

"Tell him, Mother! Tell him everything!"

A nasty smile lit up Raymond's face as he glared at the maid. "So, I was right. You do know where she is!"

"No—I—"

At her denial, he struck quickly, hitting her harshly and leaving her daughter screaming and weeping inconsolably. Mary tried to get to her mother, but he grabbed her and restrained her.

"Do I have to beat your daughter, too, to get the truth out of you?"

His threat finally broke Sylvia's will.

She could have borne up under his abuse, but the thought of his filthy hands on Mary devastated her.

"All right—all right—Let my daughter go!"

Raymond shoved the girl to the floor and closed in on the maid.

"Tell me everything! Don't hold anything back. Where is Destiny? I want to know now!"

"She had to get away—That Bryce—He tried to rape her—"

"Where did she go?" Raymond demanded, thrilled to finally be closing in on his runaway stepdaughter.

Sylvia was crying hysterically as she went to her daughter and took her in her arms protectively. "She's gone—Destiny's gone to Texas . . ."

Chapter Fourteen

Destiny awoke in the stillness of predawn with a start. The memory of the nightmare that had haunted her dreams stayed with her as she struggled to bring herself back to reality. She looked at the man sleeping so peacefully beside her and found herself smiling as she put all thoughts of her past from her.

Seth was here with her.

She was safe.

She watched him as he slept, studying his lean, handsome features. Relaxed now in slumber, he was even more attractive, and she found she couldn't resist. She wanted to be back in the safe haven of his embrace, held in those strong arms. Slipping closer, Destiny pressed a sweet kiss to his shoulder, and when she lifted her gaze, she found he was watching her.

Neither of them spoke.

There was no need for words as Lane enfolded her in his embrace and drew her to him, wanting to taste of her love once more.

It was some time later as they lay together, their limbs still entwined, that Lane smiled down at her.

"I think I'm going to be awful tired today."

"Why is that?" she asked, pretending innocence, but knowing full well neither of them had gotten much sleep that night.

"Because I have this beautiful wife who won't let me get any rest."

Destiny gave a throaty laugh as she rose up to rest on his chest and gaze down at him. "Maybe you'll have to come up to the house and take a nap this afternoon . . ."

"That's sounds like a real good idea." Lane smiled wickedly as he drew her down for a kiss. "I think I'm definitely going to need one—"

"Good, because I am, too," she murmured, savoring his embrace. All thoughts of the terror of her past were gone as she lay in his arms.

Raymond had a hangover—probably his worst ever. There was no doubt about that, but as he changed clothes and shaved the following morning, the pain in his head didn't matter. All that mattered was that he'd finally found out what had happened to Destiny. He was still furious with the maid for having kept the truth hidden from him all this time, and he didn't regret for one moment having beaten her the night before. He would have beaten her sooner if he'd known it would have brought him the information he needed. And he'd threatened her daughter with even more violence if Sylvia tried to contact Destiny and let her know he was coming for her. He was certain the threat to her child would keep Sylvia quiet. The woman had learned her lesson.

He smiled grimly to himself as he began to pack his bags. He was going to pay Bryce a visit, and then he was going after Destiny. Once he caught up with her, he was going to make her pay for what she'd done . . .

Why, she could have been married to one of the richest men in town, and instead she'd decided to run off to Texas . . .

Yes.

She was going to pay.

Destiny was surprised when she woke up to find it was morning and Seth was gone from her side. The sheets where he'd lain beside her were cool, so she knew he had slipped away some time ago. She had been sleeping so soundly, she hadn't even heard him leave—and no wonder.

She smiled to herself as she thought of the passionate night she'd just spent in his arms. Though it was true her wedding had been nothing like what she'd always dreamed of, her wedding night had been even more wonderful than any of her fantasies. She had been a true innocent to the intimate ways between man and woman until last night, but Seth had shown her the beauty of loving one another, and she would cherish that memory forever. Destiny was thankful that Seth had claimed her most precious gift. Again, she realized how fortunate she'd been to escape from Bryce that fateful night.

Destiny quickly changed the sheets and then washed up. Since Seth had gotten up and gone to work on this, the day after their wedding, she would be a responsible wife and take care of her duties, too. Caroline had promised to help teach her all she needed to know about a woman's work on the Circle D, and she was ready to learn. She had a feeling cooking would probably come first.

When they'd returned from town the previous day, she'd brought the purchases from the general store upstairs. Destiny went through them now looking for her split riding skirt, the blouse she'd purchased and the boots. Today was the first day of her new life as Rebecca Rawlins, rancher's wife, and she fully intended to look the role. She found her new clothes and got dressed quickly. Then she went to stand before the small mirror over the washstand to get a look at herself.

Destiny couldn't help smiling as she studied her reflection. She bore little resemblance to Destiny Sterling, society belle. She had transformed herself into a cowgirl, and she liked the look. She just hoped Seth did, too.

Excitedly, she left the bedroom to find her new husband and see about cooking up some breakfast.

Lane was down working at the stable when one of the boys called him outside. He quit what he was doing and went to see what the cowboy wanted.

"Hey, Boss! I think your little lady is looking for you," the ranch hand told him, nodding toward the house.

Lane looked that way and stopped what he was doing to watch Rebecca walking toward him. He decided every penny she'd spent on new clothes at the store was worth it. The pink blouse she was wearing put soft color on her cheeks, and the split riding skirt and boots drew his attention to her long, long legs. He found he couldn't take his eyes off her. He went to meet her, suddenly wanting to get her back in the house and give her a kiss.

"Good morning. Sleep well?" he asked, giving her a knowing half grin.

"You know I did. I didn't even hear you leave," she answered. Right then she had the greatest urge to wrap her arms around him and never let him go. Of course, it would have been a little awkward considering they were standing there in the open and several men were hard at work nearby.

"I know."

"I was going to start breakfast. Are you hungry?"

"Starving—" He found it wasn't only food that he was hungry for.

"Give me a few minutes, and I'll cook something up for you."

She headed off to speak to Caroline about getting some eggs to fry while Lane started back to work.

Lane warned himself that he could not afford to be distracted by Rebecca. He cautioned himself to remember the real reason he was on the Circle D, but he knew their marriage and their wedding night had changed everything.

Lane looked out over the land, wondering where the other Ranger was who was supposed to be coming to help him. He wondered, too, how close Dan Cooper and the rest of the gang were to showing up. Fortunately, everything seemed peaceful for now. Lane grinned. He was hungry for a big breakfast.

It was still early when Raymond reached Bryce's home and was shown into the study. He found the other man sitting at the desk watching him with hate-filled eyes. Raymond noticed immediately that the bandages were off, and he could see the severe gash on the side of Bryce's face. Raymond knew Bryce had always prided himself on his good looks, and he was certain the other man was furious at being so scarred.

"What are you doing here?" Bryce demanded. "Have you brought me my money?"

"No—I've brought you something better than that," he answered quickly.

"Like what?"

"Like information about Destiny. I know where she is."

"If you know where she is, why don't you go get her and bring her here to me?" Bryce raged.

"It's not that simple."

Bryce glared at him. "Why isn't it that simple?"

"Because she ran away to Texas," Raymond explained.

"Texas?" Bryce repeated, surprised. He'd thought the girl was hiding out somewhere in St. Louis. He'd had no idea she would run so far away. "What's she doing in Texas?"

"From what I learned last night, she took another girl's place as a mail-order bride."

"She *what*?" The news that Destiny had preferred to travel all the way to Texas to marry a stranger instead of marrying him left Bryce utterly humiliated and still more enraged.

"That's right. The maid finally told me what happened. She took another girl's identity and went to a town called Bluff Springs to marry some man named Rawlins."

"When did she leave?"

"That very next day."

Bryce was trying to figure out if Destiny could have reached her destination yet. "We have to move, and we have to move fast."

"That's why I came straight here this morning. I'm already packed and ready to go. I didn't know if you wanted to come with me or—"

Bryce stood up and yelled for a servant. Then he looked at the other man. "I'll be ready to leave in half an hour. We have to get to Bluff Springs before she gets married."

"I know."

"There's no chance the maid will try to let her know we're coming, is there?"

"No. I took care of that."

The two men shared a look born of hatred and the desire for revenge. Within the half hour, they left Bryce's house, intent on finding the fastest way to Bluff Springs, Texas.

Lane enjoyed every bite of the fried eggs Rebecca had fixed for him.

"You're a good cook," he complimented her as he finished his breakfast.

"Why, thank you," she said, relieved that the eggs had turned out all right. "Now, if I can just learn how to make chicken like Caroline, then I think we'll be in for some good meals."

"We sure will. Now, since you've got your riding skirt on, why don't you come on down to the stable and you can start learning how to ride astride. Since you already know how to ride sidesaddle, it shouldn't be too hard for you."

"I'd like that. The Circle D is so big, I want to be able to ride out and get a look at the place."

"We can do that."

"Shall we take our nap before the riding lesson or after?" She gave him an enticing smile, almost wishing she could lure him back upstairs for a while right now.

"Woman, I'd love to take you back upstairs this very minute and spend the day there, but I've got a ranch to run." It wasn't easy to do, but he managed to control himself despite the temptation Rebecca presented. "I'll be waiting for you at the stable whenever you're ready."

Lane got up to head back to work. He wanted to kiss Rebecca, but he knew if he kissed her even once, he might not get back to work for quite a while, and he had a lot to accomplish that day.

Texas Ranger Grant Spencer took his time making the ride out to the Circle D that morning. He'd kept his identity a secret when he'd reached Bluff Springs late in the afternoon the day before and had spent the rest of the evening getting a feel for the place. He hadn't heard any mention of Lane around town, but he had heard talk about the new owner of the Circle D, a man named Seth Rawlins who'd just married a mail-order bride.

Grant wondered where Lane was and figured he would soon be finding out. He knew Lane might have hired on as a hand at the ranch, or he could be just hiding somewhere close by waiting for Cooper and the rest of the killers to show up. One way or the other, Grant figured he would catch up with Lane real soon.

He rode for the ranch, keeping a lookout for anything unusual, and hoping once he got there that the new owner might be needing another hand and he could get hired on. If Seth Rawlins didn't hire him, he would find a way to lie low until the time was right to go after the outlaws.

Jake saw a stranger riding in and went out to meet him.

"Afternoon," Jake greeted him. He'd never seen the man around before and wondered what the stranger wanted. "What brings you to the Circle D?"

"I was wondering if your boss man's around."

"He's here. Let me get him for you." Jake went back into the stable and called for Seth.

Grant heard the cowboy call his boss 'Seth,' and he knew what was going to happen next would be a real test of his acting abilities. He had never had any encounters with Seth Rawlins, but he knew the man's reputation as a killer. As he was waiting for Rawlins to come out of the stable, he found himself wondering again where Lane was.

And then he found out.

"This here fella is looking for you, Seth," Jake was saying as the two men emerged from the stable.

Lane looked up and saw Grant. He was glad the other Ranger had shown up, but he knew he had to quickly take control of the conversation so that Grant wouldn't blow his cover as Seth Rawlins.

"Grant! It's good to see you! You got my telegram?"

"Yes, I did, and I was wondering if you're still hiring?" Grant relaxed and started smiling. He didn't know how the other Ranger had pulled it off, but it looked like Lane was now Seth Rawlins.

"We can always use a good hand here on the Circle D, right, Jake?"

"That's right, Seth."

"Grant's an old friend of mine. We go back a ways."

"That must have been one fine poker hand you had to win this spread," Grant commented as he dismounted and started to tie his horse up at the hitching rail.

"It was. I'm glad I took the chance and didn't fold. Come on," Lane said. "Let me show you around and introduce you to Steve, my foreman."

"Sounds good." They started to go back into the stable. "How long have you been here?" Grant asked.

"A few weeks, but things are working out real well."

"I spent the night in town, and I heard some talk about a wedding—" Grant began, wondering if the talk had been true.

"You heard about that, did you?" Lane shot him a quick look. "Well, a man's got to settle down some time. I thought since I had the Circle D, it was time."

"When do I get to meet your little lady?"

Lane glanced back toward the house and spotted Rebecca on her way down to join them.

"I think you're going to meet her real soon." He nodded in her direction.

Chapter Fifteen

"Grant, this is my wife Rebecca," Lane began as Destiny joined them. "Rebecca, this is my friend Grant Spencer."

She looked up at the tall, broad-shouldered, dark-haired man and smiled a bit tentatively. Something about the man seemed a little dangerous, but she wasn't sure what it was. "It's nice to meet you, Grant."

"It's nice to meet you, too, Mrs. Rawlins."

"Call me Rebecca, please."

"All right, Rebecca," he said. "After your husband, here, won the ranch in that card game, he sent me a telegram and offered me a job, so I thought I'd take him up on the offer and go to work."

"Welcome to the Circle D."

"I'm glad to be here."

Grant was amazed by the situation Lane had gotten himself into. Having taken on Seth Rawlins's identity, he obviously had been forced to marry Rawlins's mail-order bride . . .

Not that anyone would have had to force him to marry Rebecca if he'd been in Lane's shoes. She was one fine-looking female. Grant wondered for a moment if all mail-order brides were this pretty. If they were, then he just might consider ordering one for himself. Grant forced his thoughts back to his reason for coming to the Circle D—the killer Dan Cooper.

Obviously, Cooper hadn't shown up yet, so he and Lane still had time to get ready for the gang, but he couldn't help wondering what was going to happen to Lane's wife once the truth came out.

It was going to be interesting, that was for sure.

Lane looked at Jake, who was working nearby. "Jake, I just hired Grant on. Why don't you take him over to the bunkhouse and get him settled in?"

"Sure thing," Jake agreed.

Grant got his bedroll from his horse and went off with the ranch hand.

"That'll be nice for you, having your friend here. How long have you two known each other?" Destiny asked.

"We worked together on the same job a few years back," Lane explained, telling himself it wasn't a lie. He and Grant had done some tracking together in the past.

"Well, if you're ready for me, I've got time now to practice my riding," she said, determined to master riding astride.

He gave her a grin. "I'm always ready for you." He saw her blush and grinned even wider. "Come with me."

He led the way into the stable.

"What are we going to do in here?" she asked, glancing around at the stalls and tack with interest.

"You're going to learn how to saddle your horse."

Destiny looked from the heavy saddle he'd picked up to where Sunny stood in her stall. Then she stepped up to take the saddle from him, eager to learn. "All right, what do I have to do?"

They went to work. He showed her how to put the saddle and bridle on her horse and then led Sunny from her stall.

"Are you ready for a ride?"

"As ready as I'll ever be," she said, both excited and apprehensive about her first time riding astride. She wondered what Gertrude would have thought of her if she'd still been at the ranch to see her mounting up for the first time.

As she put her foot in the stirrup, Seth was there, his hands at her waist to help her, and she certainly didn't protest. In fact, she enjoyed his touch, looking over her shoulder to smile at him. "Thanks."

"You're welcome," he said, stepping back.

"All right—I think I can do this," Destiny declared as she put her heels to the horse's sides and rode Sunny out into the corral at a slow, easy gait. She circled the corral several times, enjoying the improved balance and sense of freedom she had wearing her riding skirt and boots. It was definitely easier for her than trying to keep her seat while riding sidesaddle in her long riding habit back home.

Lane climbed up to sit on the top rail of the corral's fence to watch her. "You're doing fine. Tomorrow, if you're feeling adventurous, we can ride out, and I'll show you around the place. There's a big difference between circling the corral and riding the open range."

Lane knew all about the trouble a person could run into on the range. He'd faced more than his share of it over the years. There was always the danger of rattlesnakes or cougars on the trail, and he wanted her to be prepared for trouble. She had to be able to keep her seat if the horse shied or tried to buck her off.

Destiny was concentrating on riding Sunny, and when she looked up to see that Grant and Jake had returned and were sitting with Seth, watching her, she smiled at them. "One of these days, I'll take you all on in a race!"

They laughed good-naturedly.

"When we have the big festival, you just might get the chance. There's always a race and some roping competition," Jake told her.

"I don't think I'll be doing any roping," she said, smiling.

"You can enter the race for sure, and if you're riding

Sunny, you just might win." Jake knew what a fine horse Sunny was.

When Destiny finally quit for the afternoon, she was stiff and a bit sore, but she was looking forward to riding out with Seth the following day.

"I guess I'd better go find Caroline and see about starting dinner. It's a little late to try to get in a nap," she told Seth as he walked with her out of the stable.

"We'll just have to bed down early tonight and catch up on our sleep. What do you say?" he teased.

"Well, I do like the idea of going to bed early . . ." she told him, in a voice just loud enough for him to hear.

He was chuckling as he watched her make her way back up to the house, enjoying the view of her lush figure and long legs. Once she'd gone inside, he went to find Grant, who was working with Jake.

"You feel like taking a look around the place? We can ride out and see if we can find Steve. He's the foreman, and you'll be working with him most of the time."

"Sounds good to me," Grant said easily. He was anxious to have a few minutes alone with Lane to find out all that the other Ranger had learned so far about the Cooper gang's plans and to discover what had happened to the real Seth Rawlins.

It was just a short time later that they were heading out in the direction Steve had gone earlier to check stock. Lane made sure they didn't ride too far before stopping to go over all that had happened.

"All right, Lane, let's hear it," Grant urged. "And this better be good."

Lane just gave a shake of his head as they reined in. "I never thought I'd wind up in this situation—"

"You mean your 'wife'? Seems to me she's the best part of the whole deal."

"Rebecca is special, that's for sure."

"Talk in town was that you two just got married—"

"Yesterday," Lane answered. "Just about twenty-four hours after she got here."

"Did you have any idea she was coming?"

"None."

"That must have been a real exciting moment for you." Grant could only imagine how his friend had reacted when he'd been caught unaware by the arrival of his mail-order bride.

"You'll never know . . ."

Lane went on to tell Grant how he'd been tracking the gang and how Seth Rawlins had split off from the main group. "I went after the gang but lost the trail after a storm, so I decided to double back and follow Rawlins, knowing he would be coming here. I wasn't sure whether I'd catch up with him before he got to the ranch, but I did. After the shoot-out, I decided to come here in his place since no one on the Circle D had ever met Seth before. I knew I could establish myself here and wait until they showed up."

"Now, we'll be ready and waiting for them—Seth." Grant looked over at his friend. "What are you going to do with the girl? She obviously knows nothing about what's going on."

"She is an innocent in all this, and I want to keep her that way. I want her safe."

"But after this is over and she finds out you're not Seth—"

Lane was not looking forward to that moment. "She'll understand why I had to do what I did when the truth finally comes out. I'm just glad I was the one here at the ranch when she showed up. It was tricky for a while, but I hate to think what would have happened to her if I hadn't caught up with Seth when I did."

"She sure is a lucky woman."

"Let's just hope she thinks so—"

"She will. Do you have any idea when Cooper and the others are going to get here? Did Rawlins say anything before he died?"

"No, nothing. All I know is that Rawlins was supposed to come to the Circle D and set up the ranch as a good place for them to lay low when they're hiding from the law. Have you heard any news about Cooper and his men? Have they been involved in any other robberies?"

"No. They've been quiet lately."

"Which means they're probably getting ready. I've never known Dan Cooper to stay quiet too long."

Grant knew Lane was right. The outlaw seemed to enjoy all the robbing and killing he did.

"Just remember, we have to be extremely careful around here," Lane advised. "All the men in the gang know the real Seth, and if one of them rides in looking for him and finds out I'm 'Seth,' there will be big trouble—right away."

"I'm glad I got here in time to help you. We can do this. With Rawlins dead, there are only four men left in the gang."

The two Rangers fell silent as they rode on to find Steve, each contemplating the danger that was headed their way.

"What time will we go for our ride tomorrow?" Destiny asked Seth. She was just about to go upstairs to get ready for bed, and she was wondering how early she'd have to be up in the morning.

"Looking forward to it, are you?" he teased.

"Yes. I want to see more of the ranch and find out what it's like. I mean, it's so big—"

"The Circle D covers a lot of rugged land, but it's good cattle country. We'll ride out early. That way it won't be too hot for you. While we're out, there's something else I want to teach you."

"What's that?" she asked.

"You need to learn how to use a gun."

"Why?" she asked, shocked.

"You never know when you might need one, so it's best that you be prepared just in case something happens." He couldn't help thinking of Katie as he spoke. If she'd had a gun handy that fateful night . . . He pushed the memory away.

"I think tomorrow is going to be a very exciting day . . . but not as exciting as tonight." She smiled at him. "I've got a surprise for you."

"You do?" He was intrigued and glad for the distraction. "What is it?"

"It won't be a surprise if I tell you," she teased. "Wait here for just a minute. I'll call you when I'm ready . . ."

Destiny couldn't help herself. She went to him and drew him down to her for a quick, enticing kiss.

"What have you got in mind, woman?" he growled.

"You'll see—It's a wedding present from Gertrude."

"From Gertrude?" Lane wasn't sure what to expect.

Destiny left him standing there and hurried on up the steps and into their bedroom. She closed the door behind her to give her the privacy she needed. Destiny lit the lamp on the nightstand, but kept it turned down low, and then wasted little time taking off her clothes and freshening up. She donned the silken nightgown, then paused before the mirror hanging over the dresser.

She hardly recognized the sensuous-looking woman gazing back at her. The golden glow of the lamplight revealed a look of expectation on her face, and the blush-colored silk outlined every one of her lush curves. Smiling, she went to the door to call Seth.

"You can come up now—I'm ready . . ." She left the door standing a bit ajar and went to lie seductively in their bed.

"So am I," he replied as he quickly made his way up the steps, already unbuttoning his shirt in anticipation of the night to come.

His desire for her only intensified when he pushed the door open and saw her. He stopped in the doorway to stare at the vision she made. She looked absolutely gorgeous with her hair down around her shoulders, wearing the pale, silken nightgown that clung so seductively to her soft womanly curves.

Destiny was watching him carefully and smiled invitingly, asking, "Do you like Gertrude's present?"

"I love it," he told her, coming into the room and closing the door behind him.

"How much?" she asked as she lifted her arms to him.

"I'll show you how much," Lane said in a husky voice.

He wasted no time shedding the rest of his clothes and then he joined her there on the bed. Lane stretched out beside her and paused just long enough to visually caress her once again. Unable to resist any longer, he moved over her to claim her lips in a passionate, hungry kiss.

Destiny was left breathless when his lips left hers and traced an arousing path down the side of her throat. She was trembling with desire and began to move against him in restless invitation.

Lane shifted away from her just long enough to help her slip the gown off.

Destiny eagerly complied and smiled up at him, lifting her arms to draw him back down to her. The hard heat of him against her body emboldened her. She began to caress him, her hands exploring the hard-muscled width of his shoulders and back.

Enticed by her touch, Lane kissed her hungrily before shifting lower to kiss the soft, lush curves of her breasts.

The intimate touch of his lips upon her filled Destiny with the burning need to be one with him again. Lost in the heat of her passion, she whispered his name, urging him on. She opened to him and gasped in delight as he made her his own.

They came together. The flames of their need drove them on until ecstasy was theirs.

In the aftermath of their loving, Lane lay awake, cradling his Rebecca against him as she slept. He was tired. She had worn him out, but even so, sleep was proving elusive for him this night.

He finally had admitted to himself that he was falling in love with her.

The revelation was deeply troubling to him, for it had happened so fast. One minute they'd been total strangers, and now after just two days of being together, he cared about her deeply.

Lane knew he would do everything in his power to keep her safe.

He had to.

She was his wife.

Chapter Sixteen

"This is a far cry from the St. Louis riverfront," Destiny remarked to Seth as they continued their ride across the seemingly endless miles of Circle D land. They'd been riding for over an hour, and she was in awe of the vast expanse that was their property.

"Used to more water, are you?"

"Oh, yes, a lot more water, but, at least we won't have to worry too much about the spring floods around here."

"Not like the floods you're used to, anyway," he agreed, knowing exactly where he was going to take her on their way back. "Let's stop here for a while. I think it's time you had a little target practice."

She glanced over at him as he rode so tall in the saddle beside her. She had known that he'd brought along another gun and holster for her. "You really think it's important that I do this, don't you?"

"Yes. For your own safety. This is a big country, and

you need to know how to take care of yourself in case I'm not around."

"All right. If I can learn how to ride astride this quickly, I can learn how to shoot a gun," she said with confidence, reining in. She quickly dismounted and tied up her horse.

Lane dismounted, too, and got the extra gun belt from his saddlebags before leading her a good distance away from the horses. He'd brought a few tin cans along to use as targets, and he set those up for her before handing her the gun belt.

"All right. Put this on, and let's see how good you are."

She took the holster from him a little uncertainly and managed to buckle it around her waist.

"Have you ever handled a gun before?"

"No."

"Just take your time and remember never to point a gun at someone unless you plan on shooting them."

"Let's hope I never have to worry about that." She drew the gun out of the holster and weighed it in her hand, making sure to keep it pointed at the ground. "It's heavy." She was a little surprised.

"You'll get used to it. Do you want me to help you?"

"Please."

Lane came behind her and put his arms around her to help her lift the gun and steady her aim.

Destiny loved having his arms around her. She

loved the hard feel of his chest against her back and the manly scent of him so close. It would have been so easy for her to turn around and kiss him right then, but she knew this lesson was important. She couldn't let herself be distracted. She had to pay attention to what he was trying to teach her.

"Now, pull the trigger slowly."

Destiny did as she was told. The gun jerked hard in her hand, and she wasn't surprised that her shot went far wide, not even coming close to the target.

"Looks like I'm going to need a lot of practice," she admitted.

"That's what we're here for. Try again."

He helped her adjust her aim and then stepped back to wait as she got off the second shot on her own. She missed again, but she was a little closer to the target this time.

"That's better. Keep practicing. It's not easy."

And she found out he was right. It wasn't easy, and she certainly didn't have a talent for marksmanship.

"I don't think I'm ever going to have a reputation as a sharpshooter," she told him some time later when they finally decided to quit for the day.

"We can get you a shotgun, if you want," he said, grinning.

"I don't even know if I could hit anything with a shotgun," she laughed, "but at least I might come a little closer."

They mounted up and set off again. Since it was almost noon, Destiny thought they were going back to the house, but Seth surprised her.

"There's one more place I want to show you," he said.

"What is it?"

"You'll see," he replied.

He'd piqued her interest, and she rode beside him as they covered the miles to the destination he had in mind.

Destiny was enchanted by the scene before her as they came upon it—a small pond shaded by some trees.

"What do you think?" Lane asked.

"It's beautiful . . ."

Destiny quickly slipped down from her horse's back and went to stand on the bank.

Lane tied up the horses and then joined her there.

"It's so peaceful," she said, smiling up at him.

"I know. I found this spot when I was out one day right after I first got here. It's been my favorite place on the ranch ever since."

"I can see why." Hot and tired as she was, the water looked heavenly and inviting, and she couldn't resist. She looked up at him with a twinkle of mischief in her eyes. "Come on! I need to cool down a little." She sat and pulled off her boots and socks. When she had removed them, she jumped up and dared him, "Race you!"

Destiny took off at a run, leaving him behind.

But not for long.

It had been ages since Lane had done anything so carefree, but in that moment, with Rebecca, it seemed so right. He quickly yanked off his boots and socks, too, and gave chase.

Destiny was ready for him.

The minute he got close enough, she bent down and splashed him.

Lane was drenched and laughing. The cool water felt wonderful, and he dove in after her. She tried to flee, but she couldn't move fast enough to escape from him. She squealed in delight when he snatched her up and cradled her in his arms.

"I think we need to go for a swim, don't you?"

"Oh, I don't know—I can think of something else I'd rather do than swim with you . . ." Her words were enticing.

Lane let her slide from his arms down the length of his slick body, still holding her fully against him. She linked her arms around his neck and lifted her lips to his in a sensuous kiss. The kiss ignited fires in both of them that even the cool water couldn't put out.

Thrilling to the spontaneity of the moment, they drew apart just long enough to make their way back up to the water's edge and quickly strip off their clothes, tossing them up on the bank.

Destiny had to admit she was feeling a bit shy to be so unclad out in the open, but she knew that there was no one else around for miles. They'd been riding for hours and hadn't seen a soul.

They were alone in their own little paradise.

She moved back out into the water until it was up almost to her shoulders and then gestured for him to come to her.

Lane remembered the last time she'd seen him standing before her, undressed, and he smiled. He didn't have a towel with him this time. He followed her out into the pond.

Destiny was waiting for him. He took her in his arms and lifted her to him. She responded eagerly, wrapping her legs around him and kissing him hungrily. Lane needed no more encouragement. Caressed by the water, they came together.

Later, they lay side by side on the grassy bank, savoring the beauty of their time alone together.

"I know why this is your favorite place on the ranch," she said as she leaned over to kiss him sweetly.

"I like it even more now," he said in a gruffly sensual voice.

"We could just stay here, you know. You're the boss. We don't ever have to go back."

"I like the way you think, but I'm afraid someone

will come looking for us if we don't get back to the house pretty soon."

"That's a shame." Destiny sighed. "I think I could stay here with you forever."

Drawing her close for one last, long kiss, he said regretfully, "We have to go."

They got up and dressed themselves. She looked over at him as they started to mount up.

"I think I may need a nap today. What about you?"

"You are trouble, woman," he said, knowing that the thought of taking her in his arms again was all he would be thinking about on the ride back.

She laughed and rode out ahead of him, leaving him to follow.

Dan and his boys sat around their campfire, finalizing their plans.

"You think Seth is ready for us?" Ted asked.

"He'd better be. He's had a few weeks. That should be plenty of time," Dan insisted.

"So we're going to rob the stage tomorrow?" Slick asked.

"That's right. We'll hit hard and fast and then make our run for the Circle D. I'm sure Seth has a line shack all ready and waiting for us. We can stay there for as long as we have to. Nobody will ever think of looking for us there."

"How can you be so sure?" John worried. "What if

someone's on our trail, tracking us after the robbery?"

Dan looked at him in disgust. John wasn't the brightest man around. The only reason Dan kept him in the gang was because he could shoot straight and fast.

"Why do you think I put Seth in charge of the ranch instead of you, John?" Dan snarled sarcastically. "I put Seth in charge because he's smart. He'll have this all figured out. Once we get to the Circle D, we're going to disappear."

John was angry at the insult but knew better than to say any more.

"By now, I'm sure Seth's convinced everybody on the ranch that he got lucky in a card game, and he's determined to settle down and try his hand at ranching."

Ted and Slick shut up, too. They knew better than to cross Dan or try to argue with him.

Later that evening, after dinner, Lane and Grant met up to talk. They walked out past the corral to make sure no one was around.

"So how are you enjoying married life?" Grant asked. He knew of Lane's past and the reason why he'd joined the Rangers. He'd heard Lane say that he would never marry again. He wondered if the beautiful Rebecca had changed his friend's mind about taking another chance on matrimony.

"I'm liking it just fine," Lane answered. "That first

day when Rebecca showed up unannounced with her chaperone, I was shocked. It was hard to believe that anyone in the Cooper Gang was serious enough about settling down to send for a mail-order bride, but the more I think about it, the more I'm sure Rawlins was planning to use her to cover up what was really going on. If he appeared to be all settled down and serious about ranching, no one would ever suspect he was up to something else."

"It sure is going to be tough on Rebecca when all this is over."

Lane had been thinking the same thing, but no matter how much he wished he could spare Rebecca, he could think of no way to do it.

Lane looked up at him, his expression dark. "Like I said before, I'll keep Rebecca safe. That's the least I can do. And if she still wants to be my wife, I'll do the right thing by her."

"Do you think she'll want that, after you lied to her?"

"I hope she'll understand, but right now, there's no way of knowing, and I honestly try not to think about it. I'll have to deal with that situation when the time comes. Right now, I just wish I knew more about what Seth had arranged with Cooper and the rest of the gang before they parted company. I'd hoped to question him about their plans, but I never got the chance."

"Rawlins wasn't known for talking. He was known for shooting."

"And he tried."

"I'm glad you were faster on the draw than he was."

"So am I."

They fell into a companionable silence as they looked out across the land.

"What will happen to the ranch after we're done with Cooper? Who's going to take over here?"

"Since Cooper won it in that card game, it's his, but as far as we know, he has no family."

"I guess the law will have to figure that one out."

They parted company then, knowing trouble was coming their way.

Lane returned to the house to spend the rest of the evening with Rebecca. As he stepped up on the porch, he found himself wondering just how many more evenings they would have together before Dan Cooper and his men showed up.

•

Chapter Seventeen

The stagecoach was right on time as it headed for San Miguel. The trip had gone smoothly so far. With each passing mile, the driver and man riding shotgun were feeling more and more confident that they would make it safely into town with the payroll they were carrying. They were both looking forward to taking some time to enjoy themselves down at the local saloon, where they knew the liquor was good and the working girls were pretty.

But Dan Cooper and his men had heard all about the payroll coming in on the afternoon stage, and they'd made their own plans. They had already rolled some big rocks down onto the road where it narrowed to pass through some rugged terrain, and they were ready and waiting when the stagecoach came into view.

"When should we start shooting?" Slick asked Dan.

"Wait until they stop. They'll have to get down to move the rocks. It'll be easier to take them out then."

The other men heard his orders and knew he was right. It would be much easier to catch the stage driver and guard by surprise that way, and they'd be so busy moving the rocks they wouldn't have their guns drawn.

The stage driver saw the rocks in the road ahead and grew worried.

"I don't like the looks of this. There's no way to get the stage around the rocks, so I'll have to move them. You cover me," he cautioned the man riding shotgun for him as he brought the stage to a halt.

"You don't want me to help? It'll go faster if I do," the shotgun offered.

"No. I'll hurry."

"Why are we stopping?" one of the men inside the stagecoach called out.

"There are some rocks on the trail. We'll be moving again in a few minutes," the driver assured him.

But he had no more than gotten down and started to shove the first boulder out of the way when the gunfire began.

Dan and his men showed no mercy as they blasted away at the driver and guard. The man riding shotgun got off a few rounds in their direction, but he was soon taken down by Dan, who cared only about the money chest the stage was carrying. As soon as the outlaws knew both the driver and shotgun were dead, they closed in and began firing away at the passengers. At least two of the passengers were armed and tried to shoot back at them to defend themselves, but they stood no chance against the murderous Cooper Gang.

The shoot-out was over almost before it began.

Dan got to the strongbox first and dragged it down from where it had been stowed beneath the driver's bench. He took careful aim and shot the lock off. He was smiling widely as he opened the lid to find the trunk crammed with money.

"Looks like we did real good for ourselves, boys," he bragged as he started to shove the cash into his saddlebags.

The other three gunmen joined him and stuffed their saddlebags full, too. The four killers were smiling as they mounted back up.

"Let's go see how old Seth is doing," Dan said. "Let's see if he's ready for us to pay him a visit."

He put his heels to his horse's sides and galloped away.

The other men followed, and they headed in the direction of the Circle D. If all had gone as planned with Seth, they would have the perfect place to hide out until it was time to pull off another robbery.

On the Circle D, the next few days passed quietly. Destiny began to adapt to the routine of living on a ranch. With Caroline's help, she was mastering all the duties that came with being a wife—the cooking, clothes washing and housework. It was hard, time-consuming work, and she came to realize just how spoiled she'd been in her past life. She certainly had more appreciation for the lifestyle she'd had back home when her mother had been alive, but even as she harbored those thoughts, she knew this was her home now.

Destiny was outside hanging up the wash to dry when she caught sight of Seth riding back in from the range. She was surprised he was returning earlier than usual, and she was glad. During those terrifying days when she'd been on the run from Raymond and Bryce, she had never allowed herself to dream that she would find true love in her life. She had only clung to the hope of surviving, but now—with Seth—she had found peace and love.

Seth had been honest with her from the start, and she'd appreciated that honesty. He had even told her of his first marriage, and though they hadn't spoken of his first wife again, knowing about his past helped her to understand him better. She finished hanging the clothes and went to meet him.

For some reason he couldn't explain, Lane had been feeling uneasy all morning. He'd decided to ride back in and check on Rebecca. He rode up in front of the house where she was waiting for him and reined in.

"I was missing you, woman," he said as he dismounted and went to join her.

"I'm glad. Are you hungry? Would you like some lunch?"

"Sounds good. You're turning out to be a fine cook."

She couldn't help laughing as they went inside, and she stopped just inside the door to give him a quick kiss. "That's all thanks to Caroline."

He grinned. "So, maybe I should go thank her?"

"Don't even think about it, Seth Rawlins. You've got a mighty jealous wife."

He grabbed her and kissed her again. "Good."

They made their way back to the kitchen to enjoy the midday meal together. They'd just finished eating when Jake came looking for Lane.

"Steve thinks there may be some rustling going on, and he wants you to have a look," Jake explained.

"Let's go," said grabbing up his hat.

"Can I ride with you?" Destiny asked.

"Yes, but get your gun."

She hurried to put on her holster and strode out the door after him.

Grant had been working at the stable when one of the other men called out that there was a rider coming. Grant quit what he was doing and went to see who it was. His gaze narrowed as he watched the lone horseman. When the rider drew nearer, Grant realized that he was looking at a man he'd seen on a wanted poster—Ted Wilkins, one of Cooper's men. Grant fought for calm as he went to speak to the outlaw.

"Afternoon, what can we do for you?" Grant asked cordially.

"I was looking for Seth. We're old friends, and I was just passing through and thought I'd stop by for a visit," Ted said easily.

"He's not here right now. He's out working stock. I don't know how soon he's going to get back. It might not be until tomorrow."

Grant was watching his reaction carefully, but Wilkins gave nothing away.

"If he shows up tonight, tell him Fred stopped by, and I'll try to get back to see him tomorrow."

"I'll let him know."

The man rode away at an easy pace.

Grant acted like he was going back to work, but, in truth, he was watching Wilkins's every move. He waited only a short period of time after the man rode out of sight, then got ready to leave. He told one of the ranch hands he was going out to find Seth, and eventually he would, but first he had some serious tracking to do.

Grant rode after Wilkins, making sure to stay far enough back so the outlaw wouldn't see him. He would find out where the gang had camped out for the night, and then he would go after Lane. Things were turning out just as they'd hoped. They had been incredibly lucky that Lane hadn't been at the ranch when Wilkins showed up.

As Grant had suspected, the Cooper Gang had taken refuge in one of the rocky canyons that was some distance from the house. He knew it was a safe place for them to camp out until 'Seth' gave them a more comfortable hiding place.

Confident that the outlaws wouldn't be going anywhere that night, Grant went in search of Lane. It was time for them to go to work.

Grant was grimly determined not to give up as he searched for Lane, and he finally found him riding back to the ranch with Steve, Rebecca and a few other hands.

"Grant," Lane asked right away. "Is something wrong back at the house?"

"You had a visitor today, and I thought you'd want to know as soon as possible. A man named Fred stopped by to see you."

Lane could tell just by the tone of Grant's voice exactly what had happened at the ranch house while he'd been away. "Did he say what he wanted?"

"Just that he'd be back tomorrow."

"Do you know where he's staying?" Lane asked, trying to make the question sound casual.

"I do, and that's why I thought I'd better come and find you to let you know he was in town."

"Seth—" Destiny heard the unusual edge in her husband's voice and sensed that something strange was happening. "What's going on? Who is this Fred?"

"Someone I've been hoping to hear from for some time now," he answered elusively.

"How did things go for you?" Grant looked at Steve, wanting to change the subject for the time being. "Did you find any sign of rustling?"

"No. Nothing definite," Steve told him, "but we're going to have to keep a close watch on the herd."

Lane picked up their pace now. He was in a hurry to get back to the house. He and Grant were going to leave right away, and they had a lot to do. From the way Grant had told him about the man's 'visit,' Lane was certain he'd tracked the outlaw to where the gang was camping out for the night. He and Grant had no time to lose.

Steve and the other men said nothing. They had no idea of the identity of the man who'd been looking for their boss, and they didn't care. They were just glad they hadn't found any rustlers on the Circle D, and they were hoping to get back to the cookhouse in time for dinner.

Lane's mood was grim as he considered what was about to happen. Soon, real soon, Rebecca was going to learn the truth. He was trying to figure out the best way to explain everything to her. He felt she deserved to know the truth before he rode out with Grant. Telling her wouldn't be easy, but he didn't want to leave her behind at the ranch not knowing what was really going on.

They reached the ranch house just as darkness was settling over the land.

Destiny went inside, while Lane stayed outside to speak with Grant. Grant explained how Wilkins had been the one to ride in, looking for Seth.

"I take it you tracked them down."

"I did."

"How far away are they camped?"

"They're in that canyon near the spring."

"So it's going to be hard sneaking up on them . . ." Lane was thoughtful as he considered the terrain. He'd tried to familiarize himself with the lay of the land since he'd come to the Circle D, and he had ridden out to the canyon several times.

"It won't be easy, that's for sure."

"We knew from the start it wouldn't be," Lane agreed, his determination never wavering.

"How soon do you want to be ready to ride?"

Lane looked toward the house, knowing Rebecca was inside waiting for him. "We'll leave in an hour."

"I'll be waiting for you."

The two men parted company. Grant did not envy Lane the conversation to come.

Lane went into the house and heard Rebecca working in the kitchen. He went to talk to her and found her already starting to fix dinner. He paused in the doorway, trying to think of the best way to handle the conversation, and he knew there was no 'best' way.

"Rebecca—"

She stopped what she was doing to look over at him. She wasn't sure what he wanted, but the tone of his voice warned her he had something serious on his mind. She stopped what she was doing. "What's going on, Seth?"

"We have to talk." He stepped into the room.

She eyed him warily, puzzled by his mood and uncertain of what was to come. "What do you want to talk about?"

"Why don't you sit down," Lane suggested.

She moved to sit at the table and watched him as he took a chair across from her. His expression was guarded, and the dark, unreadable look in his eyes left her decidedly uneasy. She had a feeling this was all related to the news that Grant had brought when they were riding in.

"There's something you need to know," he began.

Destiny waited.

"Grant and I will be leaving in about an hour."

"Why?"

"We have to go find 'Fred.'"

"But it's dark. Grant said he'd come back tomorrow. What's so important that you have to go find him at this time of night?" she asked, confused.

"Because his name isn't really Fred. His name is Ted Wilkins."

"Why would he lie about his name?"

"He's not the only one . . ." Lane knew this was the time to tell her the truth.

Destiny stiffened, her eyes widening in complete shock. *Oh, no! He's knows . . .* "Seth, what are you talking about?" She tried to remain calm as she waited for him to accuse her of marrying him under false pretences.

"Rebecca," he said slowly, "my name isn't Seth Rawlins. My name is Lane Madison, and I'm a Texas Ranger."

Chapter Eighteen

Destiny stared at him wordlessly.

He had been lying about his identity?

He wasn't Seth?

Shock ran through her.

Lane saw how stunned she was, and he got up and left the room for a moment. When he returned, he had his Ranger badge, and he pinned it on his shirt.

"Here's the proof if you don't believe me."

"You're a lawman?" she breathed.

He was a Texas Ranger named Lane Madison—

How could that be?

She was married to Seth . . . or was she?

"I don't understand—" She frowned as she continued to stare at the badge he now wore.

"The man who came to the ranch today is an outlaw. His real name is Wilkins, and he's part of the Dan Cooper gang, just like Seth Rawlins was."

Her eyes widened even more at his use of the word

'was.' She swallowed as she lifted her tormented gaze to his. "*Was*?"

"The real Seth Rawlins was a cold-blooded murderer. He's dead."

"Seth was a killer . . . ?" Again, she was totally lost—and horrified, as she tried to make sense out of what he was telling her. She had come to Texas to marry an outlaw?

"Yes, he was."

"And he's dead now?"

"Yes."

"But why did he send for a mail-order bride if he was an outlaw?"

"Marrying a mail-order bride would have been a cover for him. He planned to use the ranch as a hideout for the gang, and he figured settling down with a wife would make him look like an upstanding member of the community."

Destiny was shaken by this news, but at the same time, she realized what Lane had saved her from. "I almost married an outlaw—"

"Fortunately, you didn't marry him." As Lane spoke, he was more grateful than ever that he'd been the man waiting at the ranch when she'd arrived. She was an innocent, and when he even thought about what might have happened to her in Rawlins's hands, it angered him. "You married me."

"But—Lane—" She said his name tentatively for the first time. "How did you end up here?"

He knew how shocked she was, and he wanted to clear everything up for her before he and Grant had to leave. "The Cooper Gang is a deadly group of killers. They're responsible for a lot of robberies and murders in these parts. I tracked them to Black Rock, and . . ." He went on to explain all that had happened. "I cornered Seth on the trail one night, and when he went for his gun—"

Destiny knew then that her husband—Lane—had shot the outlaw in self-defense. She had never been exposed to the Wild West before, but she knew the man sitting across the table from her was a true hero. If he hadn't taken Seth's place, there was no telling what would have happened to her.

"Oh, Lane . . ."

Lane went to her and took her in his arms. "I know this is hard for you—And Grant and I—"

She looked up at him quickly, worried about his safety now that she knew the truth about him. "Where are you and Grant really going?"

"Cooper and his men are here on the Circle D. Grant followed Wilkins after he left, and he found out they're camped up near the canyon. They don't know Grant trailed Wilkins, and they don't know anything about me taking Seth's place. Grant's a Ranger, too."

"So that's why he showed up like he did . . ."

"He rode in to help me, and we're going after the gang now—tonight."

"No, you can't! They're killers, and there are only two of you. You might be hurt or even . . ." She broke off, not wanting to put her worst fear into words.

He couldn't help giving her a wry grin. "I'm a lawman. It's my job."

Destiny was overwhelmed by the revelation that the man she'd married was a Texas Ranger. Knowing she was on the run for what she'd done to Bryce, she was completely uncertain of her future. She had suffered through some hard times in her life, but nothing came close to the heartache she was experiencing now.

She loved this man—She loved Lane—And yet . . .

"Kiss me, woman," Lane said, bending to capture her lips in a tender exchange. He knew his revelations had all been a big shock for her, but he hoped he could make things right for her once he was done with the gang.

In that moment, in his arms, Destiny forgot all about the torture of her past. She gave herself over to his embrace, thinking only of her life now and what she hoped was her future with Lane. Surely her stepfather would not be able to track her all the way to Bluff Springs. Lane need never know about her past. She linked her arms around his neck and returned his kiss full measure.

"What are we going to do?" she asked breathlessly when they ended the kiss and moved apart. She knew their life on the ranch would completely change once the truth about his identity was known.

"We'll worry about that when I get back."

"But I don't want you to go—"

"I have to."

The tone he used let her know that nothing would deter him, so she said no more.

She knew she had to tell him before he left her. "I love you, Lane."

He gazed down at her and said, "I love you, too, Rebecca."

He kissed her one last time and then drew away. He had to concentrate on the job before him.

"Now that I know for sure Cooper and his men are close by, I want to make certain you're safe. Let's go find Steve and Caroline."

They walked down to the foreman's house and went in to talk to them.

Steve looked at him in amazement as Lane explained who he really was and what was going on.

"I know I can speak for the rest of the men when I say we're real glad you're the one who showed up here," Steve said with great respect. "Do you want any of us to ride with you tonight?"

Caroline looked up at her husband, fear shining in her eyes as she thought of him going after a gang of outlaws.

"No," Lane answered quickly. "I appreciate your

offer, but I need you and the boys to stay here and keep Rebecca safe."

"You're sure?" Steve was more than ready to help this man who had become his friend in such a short time.

"Grant and I will handle it."

"All right." Steve looked at Rebecca. "We've got an extra bedroom. Why don't you plan on staying here with us this evening?"

"Thank you," Destiny said.

"We're in this together," Caroline put in. Then she told Lane with a smile, "I always knew there was something special about you."

"Why, thank you, ma'am."

"No, thank *you*, Ranger Madison," she countered, and then she took charge. "Come on, Rebecca, let's go up to the house and get what you need to spend the night."

The women left, and Lane and Steve walked outside to stand on the porch and take a look around.

"It's still quiet here," Steve remarked.

"And I plan to keep it that way."

The two men shared a knowing look, for Steve had heard all about the Cooper Gang.

Lane went on. "Grant and I will be back as soon as we can. Keep her safe for me."

They shook hands. "I will."

Lane headed back up to the house, knowing it was almost time to meet Grant. Rebecca and Caroline had just come down the stairs carrying her things, and they waited for him in the front hall. Caroline went on outside to give them a moment alone.

And Lane took full advantage of it.

He kissed Rebecca passionately one last time and then said, "There's one more thing you'll need to keep with you while I'm gone."

"What's that?" She looked up at him innocently, unaware of the direction of his thoughts.

Lane went into the study and got her gun and holster out of the gun case. After what had happened with Katie, he wasn't taking any chances. "Here. I wouldn't put anything past Cooper, so be ready for trouble, just in case."

She looked up at him, her mood serious as she told him, "Lane—I love you."

"I love you, too," he said, gazing down at her. "And I'll be back."

"You'd better be," she told him fiercely. "I'll be waiting for you."

He heard Grant ride up to the house just then and knew it was time to leave. He quickly gathered up his rifle, extra ammunition and the rest of his gear and went outside to get ready to ride.

Destiny was standing on the porch desperately wanting to go into his arms and hold onto him and never let him go, but she knew he had a job to do and nothing would stand in his way. She watched as he mounted up and then went to stand near him.

He looked down at her one last time, committing her beauty to memory.

"Be careful," she whispered.

"We will."

Caroline came to stand by her side and put a supportive arm around her shoulders to draw her away. They watched the two Rangers ride off. Caroline could feel Rebecca trembling, and she gave her friend a reassuring hug.

"He's a Ranger. He'll be back."

Destiny nodded, unable to speak.

"Let's go out to the house."

Caroline led her away, helping her carry her things. She noticed the holster Rebecca was holding and understood why Lane had given it to her. If the Cooper Gang was around, these were dangerous times. She knew Steve had already gone to warn the men.

As they walked away, Destiny looked back one last time in the direction Lane had gone, but he had already disappeared into the darkness.

It was much later that night, while Destiny lay in the bed at the foreman's house unable to sleep, that she finally gave in to the torrent of emotions tearing at her heart. She hid her face in the blanket to muffle the sound of her weeping as she began to cry. Through her tears, she offered up a prayer.

Lane had to come back to her.

She loved him.

Chapter Nineteen

"Well, boys, tomorrow night we'll be sleeping in some real beds," Dan Cooper announced as he handed Slick the bottle of whiskey the men were sharing around the campfire.

"If Seth's got everything set up right," Slick Meade agreed, taking a deep drink. He hoped their friend had made comfortable arrangements for them.

"He will have. All he had to do was show up and get married. How hard was that to manage?" Ted Wilkins laughed.

"I wonder what his 'little lady' looks like? I ain't never seen no mail-order bride," John Harris said drunkenly. "Think he'll be wanting to share her with us?" John was a fool when he was sober, and he only got more stupid when he was drunk.

Dan looked over at him in disgust. "Don't even think about trying anything with Seth's wife. We've got to keep things quiet around here. We don't want anyone besides Seth to know where we are."

"All right, all right," John said, still having enough sense left to know he had to shut up whenever Dan talked to him that way.

Dan took the bottle back and enjoyed another deep drink. "Yeah, I think we'll stay here for a week or two and just take it easy for a while."

"Sounds good to me," Slick agreed.

They continued to drink for a while longer, then Dan ordered, "John, you go keep watch tonight."

"Why do I have to do it?" he whined. "There ain't nobody going to bother us here. We're safe."

"You're going to do it because I said so," the outlaw leader answered, giving him a dirty look across the campfire.

John shut up. He staggered to his feet and grabbed up his rifle. He knew better than to argue with Dan, especially after they'd all been drinking. He moved unsteadily up the hillside. He picked a spot among the rocks where he could keep an eye on things but where he would be well enough hidden from view that he could also fall asleep for a while without Dan seeing him.

Dan, Ted and Slick shared a few more rounds from the bottle and then were more than ready to bed down around the campfire. They'd been riding hard these last days to put as many miles between them and the site of the stage robbery as they could. Now, safe on the Circle D, they were going to let their guard down and get some much-needed rest.

* * *

Under the cover of darkness, Lane and Grant rode across the long miles to the outlaws' camp. They knew they had to be cautious. Cooper and his men hadn't stayed alive this long by being careless.

"There—" Grant pointed out the faint glow of the outlaws' campfire in the distance.

"We'd better leave the horses here and go the rest of the way on foot," Lane said. "I'm sure he's got a lookout posted somewhere who's keeping an eye on things."

The two Rangers reined in and left their horses behind, bringing their rifles and a rope with them. They'd already decided to try to take the outlaws that night. They would definitely have the advantage over them by attacking at night and catching the gang off guard.

Lane and Grant stayed together as they silently approached the canyon. When they'd moved in near enough that they could see the outlaws sleeping around the campfire, Lane also spotted the lone gunman positioned among the rocks on the hill just above the campsite. He pointed the man out to Grant, and they knew what they had to do. They had to take care of the lookout first. Positioned as he was, he would have clear shots at them if they tried to go into the camp.

John was disgusted and resentful as he struggled to stay awake. He knew there was no one around. Seth had taken care of everything. Being sent up there to keep watch was just a waste of time, so he put his rifle down and leaned back, trying to get comfortable against one of the big rocks. It wasn't easy, but he managed to relax a little bit, and relaxing that little bit was all it took. Drunk as he was, John passed out.

Lane and Grant split up, each circling around to close in on the man keeping watch. They moved in silently and were glad to see that the outlaw appeared to be sound asleep. Grant was closer to the sleeping man, so Lane drew his gun and kept watch over the gang at the campsite, while Grant went to take care of the lookout. He moved in quickly and knocked the man unconscious before he even had a chance to stir. Grant disarmed him, gagged him, and bound his wrists and ankles with the length of rope he'd brought along.

That done, the two Rangers were ready to take on the real trouble—Dan Cooper and the rest of his killers. Cautiously, with their guns drawn, they made their way down to the campsite. They knew how cold-blooded Cooper was, and they couldn't afford to make any mistakes. Lane and Grant moved apart and stayed back in the shadows of the night. They didn't want to give any of the outlaws a clear shot if one of them did happen to wake up.

Dan stirred and opened his eyes to stare off into the darkness. He was feeling uneasy. He didn't know why. He just sensed something was wrong, and he hadn't managed to stay alive this long by not trusting his instincts. He rolled over and sat up, wanting to check on John and make sure he was awake and keeping watch.

"John!" he called up to the lookout.

John didn't reply, but a voice did come to him out of the night.

"He won't be answering you, Cooper. And don't go trying anything. We've got you surrounded," Lane said in a harsh voice.

"Ted—Slick—" Dan yelled.

The other two gunmen sat bolt upright at his shout. They drunkenly groped for their guns among their blankets, but they immediately went still when Grant ordered them to stop.

"One more move, and you're all dead men—" Grant called out.

"What do you want?" Dan demanded, but he knew they were dead men, no matter what, and he wasn't about to surrender to anyone. He didn't know who'd tracked them down. It could be the law or bounty hunters, but either way, he was going to put up a fight. Dan still had one hand under his blanket, and he carefully slid his gun from its holster.

"We're Texas Rangers, and we're going to take you in," Lane said slowly.

Dan jerked his gun free and fired in the direction of the voice as he scrambled to try to escape into the night. "Run, boys! We ain't got no cover!"

Slick and Ted tried to get off some shots to cover their attempted escape, but the liquor had slowed their reaction time. Lane and Grant fired first. Their bullets found their marks, and the two men collapsed and lay still.

Dan was firing wildly as he tried to make it to the rocks to hide.

Lane aimed and fired a shot in his direction. Lane saw the outlaw leader fall, but then Cooper got back and kept going. Lane had always heard he was a hard man, and he knew he was facing a deadly enemy.

"You check them," Lane told Grant. "I'm going after Cooper."

Grant ran to Slick and Ted, and he was glad to find their shots had hit the mark. These two killers wouldn't be hurting anyone ever again. Certain that they were dead, he followed after Lane to back him up. He was determined to help Lane find the cold-blooded murderer who ran the gang. The gunman was still out there somewhere, and he and Lane were not going to let him get away.

Lane stayed low as he moved through the darkness. The outlaw leader was wounded, for Lane could see the trail of his blood on the ground as the lowlife tried to crawl away among the rocks. Wounded or not, Dan Cooper was still a dangerous man, so Lane took no chances.

In all his life, Dan had never been this desperate

before, and he cursed John under his breath as he sought some kind—any kind—of hiding place.

They had thought they were safe on the Circle D with Seth in charge.

They had thought Seth was going to take care of everything.

Dan had no doubt now that something must have happened to Seth.

The fact that the two men after him were Rangers convinced him of that and made him even more frantic. He knew if he wanted to stay alive, he had to move and move fast. Bleeding heavily as he was from his shoulder wound, it wasn't easy, but he found the strength to keep going. He was just glad he could still handle his gun. He dragged himself onward, knowing the cover of night was his only protection right now—that and his revolver.

But Lane was too good at tracking. He was closing in on Dan, and when he caught sight of the man wiggling into a tight space between some rocks, he shouted out, "Give yourself up now, Cooper."

"Never!" the outlaw screamed back, firing blindly in the direction of the Ranger's voice.

Lane said no more. He climbed over several of the boulders and positioned himself to be ready and waiting when the outlaw came crawling out of the narrow space. Lane realized the gunman might decide to hide in there, but it didn't matter.

Either way, he had the upper hand—Dan Cooper was trapped like the animal he was, and Lane was going to make sure the killer didn't escape.

Dan huddled in the hiding space.

He wasn't used to being afraid.

He was always the one in power.

He was always the one in control.

Anyone who defied him—died!

Rage burned within the outlaw. How had the Rangers found him? How had they known to come to the Circle D? He thought back to the night when he'd won the ranch in that card game and wondered who had told the law about his plan. He swore right then that if he lived through this night, he was going back to that saloon to find the ones responsible and make them pay.

The thought made the outlaw smile evilly, but first he had to survive this night. He leaned back against the boulder and drew a ragged breath. He knew he wasn't safe there. He had to keep moving. Drawing on what little strength he had left, he started to crawl out the opening. He was going to try to make a run for it while it was still dark.

Dan had just crawled out when he felt the cold steel of the Ranger's gun pressed against the back of his neck.

"Don't make a move, Cooper." Lane was glad his plan had worked. He had the outlaw right where he wanted him. He could see the gunman starting to shake in fear, and he smiled coldly to himself. If Dan Cooper was frightened now, he could just imagine how scared he was going to be when he saw the hangman's noose after his trial. "Now drop your gun real easy like."

Dan did as he was told, but even as scared as he was, he told himself he still had a chance to escape. The Ranger had been a fool not to shoot him right then and there. If he was that stupid, Dan was sure he could regain the upper hand. He still had the derringer he carried hidden on him all the time, and as soon as he got the opportunity, he was going to teach this fool a lesson. You didn't mess with Dan Cooper.

"Now, get up, but don't make any fast moves," Lane ordered.

Dan slowly managed to get to his feet and turned to face the man who'd trapped him there. He stared up at the Ranger holding the gun on him and knew he faced a formidable opponent.

"Let's get on back down to the campsite," Lane directed, motioning for the outlaw to move ahead of him, back the way they'd come.

Dan knew the other Ranger was somewhere close by. He couldn't afford to wait to try to escape. He had to do it right then, for he knew there was no way that he could get away from both of them.

Dan turned as if obeying the Ranger's order, but at the same time, he acted like he was stumbling so he could grab the derringer hidden in his boot. He managed to get the gun and spun around to fire.

But Lane hadn't relaxed his guard at all. He was expecting trouble from the outlaw and remained on guard. He saw the gun in the killer's hand, and he fired.

Lane watched in disgust as the gunman collapsed.

"Grant!" he called out

"I'm right here!" Grant said, running up behind him. "Are you all right?"

"Yeah."

"You got Cooper?"

Lane nodded toward the dead outlaw. "He won't be killing any more innocent people."

Lane holstered his gun.

Their job was done.

Lane and Grant dragged Dan Cooper's body back to the campsite and then brought John Harris down from where they'd left him tied up.

At first light, they were going to ride into town and turn John Harris and the other outlaws' remains over to the law.

Chapter Twenty

Destiny didn't sleep well all night. She tossed and turned, consumed by her fear for Lane's safety and by the turmoil deep within her over her hidden past. Her torment continued to deepen as she tried to figure out the right thing to do, and finally, with the dawn, she made her decision. She would tell Lane the truth about her past. He deserved no less from her. She couldn't go on living a lie, loving him as she did.

Destiny stayed in bed until she heard Steve and Caroline up and about. She gave them their privacy, and when Steve left the house, she got dressed and went downstairs to see if there was anything she could do to help her friend.

"How are you this morning?" Caroline asked when Destiny appeared in the kitchen doorway. "Did you manage to get any sleep?"

"Not really," she answered honestly. "I was too worried about Lane."

"He's a very special man. Steve and I were just talking about him. Now that we know the truth, we were wondering what's going to happen to the Circle D."

"You're right . . . Who owns it now? The outlaw won it in a card game, but . . ." Destiny realized how complicated the situation really was.

"I know. It's so confusing. And Lane is a Ranger—they're always on the move, so he probably couldn't take over even if he found a way to buy it on his own."

"But he's so good at ranching."

"Yes, he is. Steve and the boys have really come to respect and admire him since they've been working for him. I just hope the ranch doesn't end up getting auctioned off and being bought by some fool. We already had one fool for an owner with Chuck."

"Is he the one who lost the Circle D in that card game to Dan Cooper?"

"Yes. He was no ranching man. He was downright stupid, and then to lose this beautiful place in a poker game . . ." Caroline paused to look out the window as the morning sun cast its glow upon the land. "Well, that just shows you what kind of man Chuck was—losing it to an outlaw like Dan Cooper."

"We were both very blessed that Lane showed up when he did," Destiny said. "Why, if the real Seth Rawlins had been here, who knows what would have happened to all of us when Dan Cooper showed up—"

"I know, and I keep thinking, too, of you ending

up married to a vicious killer through no fault of your own." Caroline turned back to look at her.

"Sometimes I think Lane is my guardian angel—It's amazing how we ended up together, isn't it?"

"Yes, it is. The way Steve and I met was far from being that romantic. We've known each other practically our whole lives."

It had been so long since Destiny had had a close girlfriend, she was truly enjoying this time with Caroline. A part of her longed for Caroline's womanly advice on what to do about her own secret, but she resisted the desire to tell her. She kept her true identity to herself. She would tell Lane when the time was finally right.

"And Caroline—" She decided to bring up another dilemma that was haunting her. "You know the reverend in town real well—What do you think he's going to say about our wedding vows?"

Caroline could tell Rebecca was deeply troubled, and she hurried to reassure her. "I'm sure he'll say you two are married, no matter what names you used."

"Do you really think so?"

"Yes, but we can always talk to him as soon as Lane gets back just to make sure."

Destiny nodded and looked up, her gaze meeting Caroline's.

"When Lane gets back . . ." Destiny repeated, finding herself praying once again that he would be back—and soon.

To distract herself, she got busy helping Caroline, but even so, Lane never left her thoughts.

With each passing mile spent in the hot, filthy stagecoach, crowded against other passengers who were loud and obnoxious, Bryce's disgust and fury with Destiny grew. She had rejected him in favor of marrying a complete stranger and coming to live in this godforsaken land. His outrage over her insult was intense, and his need for revenge burned inside him. He noticed Raymond watching his face, and he turned to glare at him.

"What are you looking at?" Bryce demanded in a snarl.

"Nothing," Raymond said and hastily looked out the window of the stage. His days of traveling with Bryce had been awkward and strained, and as they drew ever closer to the moment when they would finally catch up with Destiny, he wondered what was going to happen. It was obvious Bryce wanted revenge, but Raymond wasn't sure just what his 'revenge' would prove to be, and he certainly couldn't ask.

Bryce stared unseeingly at the elderly woman sitting across from him in the stagecoach. His thoughts were consumed by what he was going to do to Destiny when he found her. The trip had taken longer than he'd hoped, and there was a good chance she would already be married to the stranger. The thought that she'd given her virginity to someone else enraged him, but he told himself that ultimately, that didn't matter. What mattered was revealing her disguise and getting her back to St. Louis with him. He would still marry her, and, once they were married, he was going to take great pleasure in forcing her to his will every day of their married life. She was going to learn just how dangerous it was to defy him. No one who did ever got away with it. His reputation as a vicious adversary was proof of that.

Bryce noticed that the old woman was watching him, giving him a slightly uneasy, tentative smile, and he actually allowed himself to smile back at her. It was his first smile in a long time, but he had reason to smile. He was soon going to get his revenge.

Raymond didn't notice anyone else on the coach. He was caught up in worrying about what was to come. The stagecoach was getting close to Bluff Springs. It wouldn't be long now before they would actually be coming face to face with Destiny. He tried to keep himself from trembling as he imagined what Bryce was going to do. Whatever it was, it wasn't going to be pretty. Raymond didn't really care what happened to Destiny. He just hoped he could get out of his debt to Bryce and go on with his life.

Marshall Westlake sat at his desk in his law office, staring at the other lawyer sitting before him. There was a determined look in his eyes as he waited for the man to answer. "Well?"

Stanley Atkins seemed decidedly uneasy. "Well . . ."

"I asked you a question, Atkins. Did you witness Mrs. Sterling's signature on the new will?"

Stanley decided there was no point in stalling. Westlake had a reputation for getting to the truth, and there was no way for him to cover it up any longer. "No, I did not witness her signature on the will."

"Then, would you agree with me in saying this document is a forgery and not the true will of the Sterling estate?"

"Yes."

"Good. The Sterling estate belongs to Destiny Sterling. Isn't that right? Raymond Howard has no control of the family's fortune."

"Yes."

Marshall stood up and showed the man from his office. He wanted nothing more to do with him. Now he just had to find a way to locate the missing Sterling girl and set things straight.

It took Lane and Grant a while to reach town, but they arrived just as the businesses of Bluff Springs were opening their doors. They went straight to the sheriff's office and turned John Harris and the other outlaws' remains over to the lawman. They watched in satisfaction as the sheriff locked the lone surviving member of the gang in the jail cell. When that was done, the sheriff sent his deputy to get the undertaker.

"I can't believe you did this, boys!" Sheriff Langston declared as they waited for the undertaker to show up. "When the word gets out that you've brought the Cooper Gang in, folks in these parts are going to celebrate! Why, did you hear about the stage robbery the gang just pulled off? They killed everybody on the stage and stole the payroll that was being transported."

"We've got the payroll," Lane informed him, throwing the outlaws' saddlebags on his desk. Lane and Grant hadn't known what the outlaws had robbed, but they'd known it had to have been a big job to get that much money. "You might want to have the banker lock those up for now." He gestured to the cash-filled saddlebags.

The lawman looked at the two Rangers standing before him. "We'll do just that as soon as the deputy gets back with the undertaker."

A half an hour later, when the deputy had returned and the undertaker had taken the outlaws' bodies away, the sheriff was ready to head to the bank with the Rangers.

"Come on." He picked up the saddlebags. "Let's go see the banker, and then we'll stop by the saloon on the way back, and I'll buy you a drink. This deserves some celebrating."

Lane and Grant smiled. "That sounds like a fine plan."

Sheriff Langston left his deputy in charge, and the three men went to secure the cash from the outlaws' last robbery. After stopping at the bank and filling out the necessary paperwork, they headed for the saloon and went to stand at the bar.

The bartender was always the first to know the talk around town, and when he saw them come in, he yelled out to those already there drinking, "Hey, everybody! Here they are! These are the Rangers who brought in the Cooper Gang!"

Though it was still early in the day and the bar wasn't crowded, the cheer that went up was a loud one.

"Your drinks are on me," the bartender told Lane and Grant as he poured them each a healthy glass of whiskey. "And you, too, Sheriff."

"Thanks," Lane said as he picked up his glass.

"We appreciate it," Grant agreed.

"No, thank *you*," the bartender said, his tone growing serious. "Our lives will all be a lot safer now that those killers aren't running free."

Some of the other men in the saloon heard his remarks and called out their agreement with him.

The sheriff enjoyed one drink with the Rangers before leaving to return to work.

Lane and Grant took their glasses and went to relax for a few minutes at a quiet table.

"We need to send a telegram to the captain before we head back to the Circle D," Lane remarked thoughtfully. His mood was growing troubled as he tried to sort out his future.

"What's bothering you?" Grant asked. He knew his friend too well not to notice the change in him.

"Well," Lane began, looking up at him, "I've got a lot to straighten out when I get home."

Grant grinned. "Your little lady?"

He nodded in response.

"What are you thinking?"

"It may be time for me to quit being a Ranger. After these last weeks living on the Circle D, I've found that I miss ranching."

"You don't think that little gal of yours has anything to do with this, do you?" Grant asked, troubled that Lane would think about quitting. He was a good and honorable man, a fine Ranger.

"I know she does," Lane admitted. "And there is one more stop I have to make besides the telegraph office—"

"Where is that?"

"I need to go by the church and speak to the reverend."

Grant frowned. "Why?"

"I want to find out if our marriage is real. Since I was lying about my name, the ceremony may not be valid. I don't want to make things any harder on Rebecca than they already are."

"It'll be interesting to see what he has to say. What are you going to do if he tells you you're not really married to her?"

Lane's expression was serious as he answered, "I'll have to ask her to marry me all over again and get her back to the altar as fast as I can."

"Good luck."

Both men laughed.

"What about the ranch? What's going to happen to the Circle D? Cooper won it—Seth was just acting the part of owner."

"I know. I've never heard that Cooper had any relatives, so it'll depend on what the sheriff wants to do. He'll probably auction the place off."

"Have you got enough money to buy it?"

"I've got some cash put away."

"Then talk to the sheriff about it, and seriously think about buying the Circle D. I've heard the ranch hands talking about you. They respect you, and they liked how you were running things."

"I think, first, I'd better talk to Rebecca."

"You're a wise man, Lane Madison." Grant laughed.

"That's why I'm going to stop by the church right after we send that telegram."

"What are we waiting for?"

"Let's get going." Lane wanted to return to the ranch as quickly as possible. He knew Rebecca was worrying, waiting to hear what had happened, so the sooner they got back, the better.

They finished their drinks and headed out.

A short time later, Lane was at the church waiting to speak with the reverend. Grant had decided to wait outside so that Lane could speak privately with the minister.

"Good afternoon—Ranger Madison—" the reverend greeted him warmly. "What can I do for you today?"

"I see you've already heard about who I really am and why I was here—to catch the Cooper Gang?"

"Yes, word came to us right away. You did a very brave thing."

Lane just nodded. "I have a serious question for you—"

"Yes?" He waited expectantly.

"It's about Rebecca—and our marriage—"

"What about it?"

"Well, since I didn't use my real name when we were married, is our marriage valid, or should we take our vows again?"

"I believe your marriage is a real one. You both stood before the Lord and took your vows. You are man and wife. But if you would like to take your vows again using your true name, I'd be more than happy to oblige, and I can issue a second marriage certificate with your real name on it. That would be best in the eyes of the law."

"I thought so."

Lane thanked him for his counsel and went out to join Grant.

"Let's go home," Lane said.

"What did the preacher say?" Grant asked.

"I've got a wife waiting for me," Lane responded.

They were both smiling as they rode out of town.

Chapter Twenty-one

As Lane and Grant approached the ranch house, the sun was shining and it was a beautiful day.

"Have you made up your mind? What are you going to do?" Grant asked. Lane had been quiet for most of the ride to the Circle D, so Grant had known he was doing some serious thinking.

"I think I have," Lane said as they reined in on top of a low rise near the house. He stared down at the scene below, and in his heart he knew this was where he wanted to be.

"So you're going to get serious about ranching, are you?" Grant glanced over at him.

"First, Rebecca and I have to talk. I'm sure she's going to have a few things to say about everything that's just happened, but I want to make our marriage work, and I want to stay here. The Circle D is a good ranch, and the hands are hardworking. They love the place, too, and if I can keep things going, it'll be good for all of us. What about you?" Lane knew he'd have to send another telegram to the captain once he and Rebecca had decided on their future.

"I'll move into town later today to wait for my next assignment."

"You're welcome to stay here and work with me," Lane offered, slanting him a sidelong grin.

"It's good to know I've got a job waiting for me if I need another one."

They started down toward the house.

"They're back!"

Destiny was up at the main house when she heard the ranch hand's call. She quit what she was doing and rushed outside to watch as Lane and Grant rode up. She didn't hesitate, but ran straight to Lane.

Lane saw her coming, and he had to smile when he saw she was wearing her holster. He quickly dismounted. He wasted no time sweeping her up in his arms and holding her close.

"You're here . . ." She sighed, looking up at him with tears in her eyes.

He didn't speak. As he looked down at her innocent beauty, he was so overcome with emotion he was robbed of words. Instead, he just bent down to her and kissed her.

The ranch hands had started to gather round, and they were all laughing and carrying on about the boss kissing his woman right there in front of them.

Lane was laughing when he broke off the kiss.

"Did you get the gang?" Steve asked, joining the other men with Caroline by his side.

"We got them," Lane answered, his tone turning serious. He didn't go into detail about everything that had happened. He didn't want to talk about it in front of the women. He and Grant would tell the men later how the shoot-out had gone down.

It was the good news everyone had been hoping to hear, and they all congratulated Lane and Grant. The hands knew the future of the Circle D was in doubt, but they were glad the Rangers were safe.

Steve looked at Lane as the commotion quieted down. He put into words what everyone was wondering. "So, what happens to the ranch now?"

"We're not sure just yet. We've still got a few things we need to straighten out in town." And Lane knew that wouldn't happen until he'd had his chance to talk with Rebecca. "I'll let you know as soon as I've got things figured out."

"Well, boys, I guess we'd better get on back to work," Steve directed.

The men moved off as the foreman had ordered.

Caroline took Rebecca aside to give her a quick hug.

"Everything turned out just fine," Caroline said, her eyes twinkling with excitement for her friend.

"Thank God," Destiny replied, her tone heartfelt as she returned Caroline's hug.

"I'll talk to you later," Caroline told her, and she went on back to finish her own chores.

Destiny looked over at Lane, who was still deep in conversation with Grant. "I take it you two could use something to eat?"

"That sounds great," both men answered.

They started up to the house.

Caroline paused on her way back to her own home to watch Rebecca and Lane together. She hoped with all her heart that they could find a way to remain on the Circle D.

As Destiny walked inside, she took off her holster and set it on the hall table. She smiled at Lane and Grant. "Now that you're back, I don't have to worry about wearing that all the time."

"No, you just have to worry about feeding two hungry men," Grant teased.

"How does breakfast sound?"

Lane knew how good she'd become at cooking breakfast, and even though it was early afternoon, he told her, "That sounds real good to me."

"Me, too," Grant added.

Destiny got right to work. She had learned during their time together how much Lane liked his fried eggs and bacon.

"I'll have to send another wire when I get into town later this afternoon and find out where I'm headed next," Grant told Lane as they finished the meal.

"Like I told you, you're more than welcome to stay here," Lane said.

"No, there's always more work to do for the Rangers. Although I have to tell you, with a good cook like Rebecca around, I'm tempted to stick around."

Lane walked Grant from the house as Destiny washed the dishes and tidied up the kitchen. He returned, more than ready to set things straight between them.

Destiny was relieved and happy that Lane had come back safely, but now she had to face what the future held for her. She had made her decision, and she knew she had to be honest with him. She had to tell him the truth about her past, and the sooner the better. As she waited for him to return, she felt increasingly nervous about what she had to say, so she kept busy, cleaning up the kitchen.

"Rebecca—"

She turned quickly to find him standing there in the kitchen doorway, watching her.

"Come here, woman."

She didn't hesitate. She went into his arms and kissed him, clinging to him tightly. "I'm so glad you're back safe. I was so worried about you . . ."

"It's over."

"Good."

He kissed her again, and then, wanting to let her know about his conversation with the reverend, he put her from him. It wasn't easy, but they had to talk. "We've got a lot to talk about."

"I know," she said tentatively.

Lane heard the uncertainty in her voice and was sure it had to do with him. He figured she probably thought he was going to return to his old job as a Ranger, that he would just ride away and never look back. He wanted to put those fears to rest right away. Taking her by the hand, he went into the parlor and drew her down beside him on the sofa.

"When Grant and I were in town, I stopped at the church to talk to Reverend Moore—"

"Oh—" She swallowed nervously, unsure of what was coming next.

"I wanted to know whether our marriage was a real one or not, since I lied about my name when I took the vows." He saw the pain in her eyes as she looked up at him, and he hurried to reassure her. "He said we were man and wife in the eyes of God, but it might be a good idea to take our vows over again so that there are no legal issues."

He opened his arms to her, and she went into them, clinging to him for a long moment.

Destiny had always felt safe and protected in his embrace, but she knew this might be the last time he ever held her this way. Once he found out the truth, his feelings for her might change completely. She had to tell him about Bryce, and she had to tell him now—before he started believing they had a future together . . .

Since he was a Ranger, Destiny suddenly wondered what he would do when he learned she had attacked a man. Would he arrest her and try to take her back to St. Louis? The thought was terrifying, but she couldn't go on lying to him any longer.

"Lane—" His name was choked from her.

He heard the distress in her voice and held her back away from him to look down at her. "What's wrong, love? If you're worried about what kind of life we're going to have, I've already been giving it some thought, and I . . ."

"No—Wait—Listen—" Utterly miserable, she pulled herself free of his embrace and got up.

The look on her face seemed to be one of sheer desperation, and Lane had no idea what was wrong. "What is it? What happened while I was gone?"

Destiny fought for control over her chaotic emotions. "What happened is that I realized I can't go on living a lie with you."

"Oh." Lane immediately thought she was furious with him because he'd lied to her. "Rebecca, I'm sorry I had to lie, but it was the only way I could do my job. I had to—"

"That's what I mean!" The words rushed from her. "You're a lawman!"

Now, Lane was really confused.

She went on, not waiting for any response from him. "You're a Texas Ranger—and I . . . I'm on the run!"

"Rebecca—" He was completely bewildered by her confession. He got up to go to her.

But Destiny put up her hand, and she backed away from him.

"No—Stop, Lane—I have to tell you this. I can't lie to you anymore."

"Lie to me anymore? You've been lying to me? What are you talking about?"

She looked him straight in the eye as she confessed, "My name isn't Rebecca Lawrence!"

"I don't understand—"

"My name is Destiny Sterling, and the law back in St. Louis is after me . . . for murder . . ."

Lane went still as he tried to come to grips with her revelation. He'd been caught off guard a number of times in his life, but this was a complete shock to him. He was quiet for a minute, watching her, trying to assimilate what she had told him.

"Tell me what happened," he said quietly, sitting back down on the sofa to listen to her story.

Destiny was trembling as she began to tell him everything. "After my mother died, my stepfather had control of my family's money, and he gambled a lot . . . He must have gambled it all away. He owed another businessman a lot of money from gambling, and this fellow agreed to cancel his debt if I married him. I barely knew him, and I didn't really like him. He was rich, but . . ." She looked up at Lane, her torment evident in her expression and the desperate look in her eyes. "I tried to tell my stepfather 'no,' but he said I had to either marry Bryce or marry *him*!"

At that memory, she began to cry.

Lane couldn't stop himself. He went to her and took her in his arms, drawing her back to sit with him again. He could feel her shaking as he held her by his side. "Go on."

"I told him I'd go see Bryce, so he took me to his house and then left me there!" The memories came flooding back. "Bryce pushed me down on the sofa and tried to rape me—I told him to stop! I begged him to stop! But he wouldn't. I was so scared I grabbed a vase that was on the table nearby, and I hit him on the head with it . . ."

She began to sob as she revealed the terrible secret she'd kept hidden all this time.

"What happened next?" Lane knew reliving the ordeal was hard for her, but he urged her to go on.

"He was bleeding, and I pushed him off of me . . . He just lay there on the floor! There was blood everywhere . . . I ran away. There was nothing else I could do . . . There was no one I could go to—I had to get away! He was dead. I killed him." She collapsed against Lane as she finally gave vent to her horror at what had happened that night.

"Are you sure he was dead?" Lane asked quietly.

"He wasn't moving—I hit him so hard the vase shattered—"

Lane said nothing for a moment. He held her in his arms, cradling her against him as she surrendered to the painful memories of her past.

Lane realized how terrible that night had been for her, but he also knew that what had happened to her was not her fault. She had acted in self-defense when she'd hit the man who was trying to rape her. And Lane wasn't quite sure he believed this Bryce was really dead.

"We'll take care of this," he said in a quiet voice, wanting to reassure her.

"But how?" she asked, looking up at him in confusion.

She could think of no way to solve her problem. After all, Bryce was dead.

"We'll go back to St. Louis, and we'll find out what really happened and clear this all up."

"But I killed him . . ."

"No. You acted in self-defense."

"Don't you have to arrest me?"

He looked her straight in the eye as he told her,

"You don't know for sure that this Bryce is dead. You might have just knocked him unconscious when you hit him. We need to go back and learn the truth."

"But you don't know how evil my stepfather is, and if Bryce is still alive . . ."

"I'm a Texas Ranger, Destiny," he said, speaking her real name for the first time. "It's going to be all right."

"Oh, Lane . . ." She collapsed against him and wept, safe in the haven of his arms. It had never occurred to her that Bryce might have been just knocked unconscious that night.

"Easy, love. I'm here. No one will ever hurt you again," he vowed to her.

Anger filled him as he thought about her stepfather and what he'd tried to force her to do. Yes, they were going back to St. Louis, and he was going to set things straight for her.

No one was ever going to take advantage of her again.

He was going to see to it.

Chapter Twenty-two

It was late that afternoon when Lane and Grant walked out of the stage office.

"So, do you think you can be ready to leave for St. Louis that soon?" Grant asked. He'd been surprised when Lane had decided to ride back into Bluff Springs with him, but during the trip to town, his friend had confided in him about Destiny's past, and then he'd understood.

"I should be able to get everything ready in two days. The most important thing I have to do now is to find out from Sheriff Langston what he plans to do about the Circle D. Steve and the boys are worried about their future on the ranch, and I want to set their minds at rest."

"So you have made your decision?" Grant glanced at his friend.

"Yes. As soon as I get back from St. Louis and everything is straightened out, I'll be taking up ranching full time."

"When are you going to tell the captain?"

"I'll have to send him a wire and let him know I'm going to St. Louis, but I won't tell him the rest until I've gotten everything worked out."

"I'll miss working with you," Grant said.

Lane smiled at him. "I already told you, you can stay on at the Circle D."

They both laughed.

"I don't think I'm ready to settle down."

For a moment, Grant wondered if the day would ever come when he would think about having a wife and family, but as quickly as the thought came, he pushed it away. Being a Ranger was his life. There was nothing else he wanted to do.

They started over to the sheriff's office.

"Afternoon, Lane—Grant—" the lawman greeted them, a little surprised to find the two men back in town so soon.

"How's Harris doing?" Lane asked.

"The doc came over and patched him up. He's resting real quiet back there. He ain't been giving me any trouble."

"Good," Grant said.

"I have something for you," Lane began, and he took a large amount of cash out of his pocket and handed it over to the sheriff. "This is most of the cash I found on Seth Rawlins after our shoot-out. I'm not sure if it's gambling money or part of some cash from a robbery, but I wanted to turn it in."

"You said 'most' of the cash?"

"Yes. I took out enough to give the ranch hands their back pay when I first got here, but the rest of the money is all there."

"I appreciate your honesty," Sheriff Langston said. "I'll make sure it's taken care of."

"Thanks, and I have one other thing I need to talk to you about."

"What is it?"

"What's going to happen to the Circle D now? I know Dan Cooper won the ranch in a card game from the previous owner. Seth Rawlins was just acting the part of the owner. It was Cooper's, and as far as anyone knows, he has no family."

"I see—" The sheriff was thoughtful. "You know anybody who'd be interested in buying it?"

"I would," Lane declared.

"I can see about auctioning it off. Let me talk to the judge and find out what I can arrange."

"I'd appreciate it."

"So you're planning to stay on here in Bluff Springs?"

"Yes. I'd like to make this my home."

"Good. We need upstanding folks like you in these parts. I'll let you know what the judge has to say about the ranch."

"Thanks."

Lane and Grant stopped outside to say their good-byes, and then Lane rode for home.

Lane was anxious to get back, knowing how upset Destiny had been when he'd left her. He hoped the time she'd had alone had given her the peace she needed to be ready to face what was to come. Their trip back East to find out the truth about her past wasn't going to be easy for her, but together they would do it.

After Lane had left to go into town with Grant, Destiny had stayed up at the house, needing some time alone to think things through. She had never dreamed she would tell anyone about her past. She'd believed she was going to have to keep the horror of it locked deep within her forever, but now Lane knew everything.

Destiny stared sightlessly out the bedroom window. She wasn't sure quite how she was supposed to be feeling at this moment. Her emotions were torn, and her thoughts were in turmoil. A part of her was flooded with relief—the relief that she had been honest with Lane and he'd been so supportive of her.

Once she'd learned he was a lawman, she'd feared he would condemn her and possibly even want to arrest her and take her in, but instead, he'd immediately defended her, wanting to find out the truth of what had happened that night in St. Louis. Until that moment, she'd never considered that Bryce might have survived—that he could still be alive—and she'd never thought of her action as self-defense. She'd only known that she had been alone in the world and had done what she'd had to do to survive.

Destiny went to sit on the edge of the bed, wondering what was going to happen when they returned to St. Louis. Her feelings of guilt over what she'd thought she had done to Bryce were still with her, but if they discovered he was alive, and she had only knocked him unconscious—that would change everything.

She thought, too, about seeing Raymond again, and just the thought of being near him sickened her. Compared to a true man like Lane, Raymond was nothing more than a weasel—a disgusting excuse for a man who had only used her mother, marrying her for her money.

Destiny didn't know how she'd been so blessed to end up married to such a wonderful man, but she offered up her thanks that Lane had come into her life, and she prayed that they would be able to work everything out once they returned to St. Louis.

It was almost sundown when Lane rode in. He told himself he was home, and it felt good. He took care of his horse down at the stable and went straight on up to the house.

Destiny had been busy cooking their dinner and hadn't heard Lane ride in. She did, however, hear him come through the front door, and she stopped what she was doing to hurry to meet him. Without a word, she went into his arms and drew his head down for a kiss.

"That sure was a nice welcome home," he told her with a grin when they finally moved apart.

"I've been waiting for you, and your dinner is almost ready." She took him by the hand and drew him into the kitchen. "Go wash up, and it'll be time to eat."

"Yes, ma'am," he teased as he went into the washroom.

As they ate their dinner together, he told her what he'd learned in town.

"I checked at the stage office, and we can plan on leaving for St. Louis two days from now."

"So soon . . ." The news was unsettling.

Lane's gaze met hers gravely as he told her, "The sooner the better. We need to find out what really happened that night."

"I know . . ." She gave him a tenuous smile.

"I also spoke with the sheriff about the ranch."

"Did he have any idea what's going to happen to it?"

"Sometimes, when there are no heirs to a piece of property, the land is auctioned off. Sheriff Langston said he thought that would probably be the case with the Circle D."

"But who's going to buy it?"

Lane met her questioning gaze. "We are."

"We are?" Hope blossomed within her.

"I have some money put away, and I'm hoping I can get a loan from the bank."

"So we're going to stay here?" Her heart lightened at the news.

"Yes."

"What about the Rangers?"

"After we get back from St. Louis, I've decided to quit. I've got a wife now. It's time for me to settle down, don't you think?" he asked her.

"Oh, Lane—"

Destiny got up from where she was sitting and went to him. Lane drew her down on his lap and kissed her deeply.

"I made you a peach cobbler for dessert," she said when they ended the kiss.

"I can think of something a whole lot sweeter that I'd like to have right now . . ."

She said no more but gave him a sensuous smile and kissed him again. They made their way quickly upstairs to the bedroom and wasted no time enjoying their dessert.

Bryce and Raymond climbed down from the stagecoach at the way station where they were going to spend yet another night.

"How much farther is it to Bluff Springs?" Bryce demanded of the stage driver.

"We should be there some time tomorrow," the driver answered.

At the news, Bryce turned and walked away. He could smell the food that was being cooked for their dinner that night, and the odor disgusted him. He was certain the beds were probably lice-infested, too. The thought of spending another night sharing a crowded room with the other men who were traveling in the coach angered him even more. The only positive thought he had was that this was their last night on the road.

Destiny slipped back into his thoughts then. Tomorrow, they would find her. Tomorrow, she would be his. He was looking forward to seeing the look on her face when she spotted him for the first time. He couldn't wait. She was going to learn what happened to anyone who dared to defy him.

That thought alone brought him some satisfaction. He stayed outside as long as he could, not wanting to be in the same room with the other men if he could avoid it. When he finally bedded down in the crowded room, he told himself it wouldn't be for much longer.

Raymond had stayed away from Bryce ever since the stagecoach had stopped for the night. He had sensed the other man's surly mood, and he didn't want to risk a confrontation with him. He'd heard the answer the driver had given Bryce about how much longer it would be until they reached Bluff Springs, and he was thrilled that this horrible trek would soon be over. Of course, they would have to travel back to St. Louis, but at least on the return trip, Bryce would be in a much better mood, for he would have Destiny with him.

Raymond lay awake most of the night in the hot, smelly bedroom, listening to the other men snoring as he tried to imagine what was going to happen when the stagecoach finally reached Bluff Springs. He wondered what kind of reaction they would get when they started asking around about Destiny and the man who'd sent for her. He knew the man's name was Seth Rawlins, so he hoped they wouldn't have too much trouble locating him. Getting Destiny away from Rawlins might prove to be difficult, but he figured Bryce would find a way to make it happen. He always got what he wanted, and Destiny would be no different.

Marshall Westlake finally managed to find the small shanty of a home where Sylvia, the Sterlings' former maid, was living with her daughter. When he'd stopped by the Sterling house to speak with the servants, trying to get more information on Destiny, the maid who was working there now told him how the other woman had quit after her run-in with Raymond.

It was late as he knocked on the door, but Marshall knew this conversation was too important to put off another day.

"Who is it?" a feminine voice called out to him from inside.

"I'm Marshall Westlake. I'm the deceased Mrs. Howard's attorney," he announced.

Sylvia had no idea why the lawyer was at her home, but she knew he was an honorable man from all that Miss Annabelle had told her over the years. "Mr. Westlake—please come in . . ." She quickly opened the door for him.

"Thank you." He stepped inside.

"What is it? What can I help you with?"

"It's about Destiny Sterling and her mother's will," he began. "I need to find out where Miss Sterling has gone."

"Please, have a seat. I'll tell you everything I know—"

Marshall sat down on the worn sofa to listen to her story. It was much later that night when he got ready to leave Sylvia. She had told him all that had happened, how her employer had attacked her and threatened her and her young daughter.

"I appreciate your confiding in me," Marshall told

her, knowing how dreadful the situation must have been for her.

"Can you find a way to help Destiny? Can you keep her safe from those terrible men?"

The lawyer looked down at her, his mood serious as he contemplated how to handle the information she'd just given him. "I'll do everything I can. I promise."

Chapter Twenty-three

It was the first morning since they'd set out from St. Louis that Raymond and Bryce were both excited. They kept their emotions to themselves, but they climbed aboard the stagecoach eagerly and watched anxiously as the vehicle crossed the seemingly endless miles toward Bluff Springs.

It was near noon when the elderly lady riding in the stage with them spotted the town in the distance. "Well, boys, it looks like we're almost to town."

Bryce looked in the direction she was pointing and got his first view of Bluff Springs. It was small, hot and dusty, and he could only imagine the misery of living in such a place so far from any real civilization. When the stagecoach rolled to a jerky stop in front of the stage office, Bryce could hardly wait to get out.

The stage driver climbed down to open the door. "We're not staying here long, folks. Those of you who are continuing on with me can get out and stretch for a while if you want. We'll be heading out again in fifteen minutes."

The passengers all climbed out, glad for the respite.

Bryce and Raymond stood next to the stage, looking up and down the main street of town as the driver tossed their bags to the ground. They noticed that some of the men from town were openly staring at them, and they realized how out of place they looked. Not that it mattered. They had no intention of staying in this pitiful excuse for a town any longer than they had to. They'd come to Bluff Springs to find Destiny and take her home.

"Where shall we start looking?" Raymond asked Bryce. "Do you want to take rooms at the hotel?"

"This town is so small, I'm sure whoever is working the desk there will be able to tell us how to find the Rawlins ranch."

They picked up their bags and made their way to the only hotel in town.

The clerk had heard the stagecoach roll in and thought there might be a customer or two for the hotel. He saw the two Eastern dudes enter the small lobby and welcomed them. "Good afternoon, gentlemen. How can I help you?"

"We need two rooms."

"Fine. That'll be two dollars—in advance."

Raymond made short order of paying him, and the clerk handed them their keys.

"Top of the steps at the end of the hall, the last two rooms on the left."

"Thanks. By the way, we're here to find a Mr. Seth Rawlins. The owner of the Circle D Ranch. Are you familiar with him?"

Both Bryce and Raymond were a little caught off guard by the change in the man's expression.

"You sure you're looking for Seth Rawlins, or are you looking for Lane Madison?" He eyed them suspiciously.

Bryce didn't like to be questioned about any of his private business, but he sensed something strange was going on. "Actually, I'm not sure who Lane Madison is, but we're relatives of Seth Rawlins's wife—Rebecca. We've come from St. Louis for a visit."

The clerk was studying the scars on the man's face, thinking he was one ugly dude, all cut up as he was. The clerk knew, too, that these men would soon find out about all the excitement that had happened at the Circle D. "Oh, all right. If you go down to the livery stable, Ol' Mick will help you. He can drive you out to the ranch."

"We appreciate your assistance."

Bryce and Raymond were aware that the clerk was watching them carefully as they proceeded up the stairs to leave their belongings in their rooms before seeing about arranging a trip out to the ranch. Each went into his own room for a moment, and then Raymond came knocking on Bryce's door.

"Come in."

Raymond walked in to find the other man standing at the window staring down at the street. When he closed the door behind him, Bryce looked his way.

"How are we going to handle this once we get out to the ranch?" Raymond asked, growing a little uneasy now that the moment had come.

"That's up to you. I don't care how you do it. You're Destiny's stepfather. I just want her heading back to St. Louis with us on the next stagecoach out of town," Bryce ordered with a threatening glare.

Raymond nodded nervously. "Then let's go get it over with. This isn't going to be a warm family reunion, that's for sure."

They left the hotel and made their way to the stable.

Ol' Mick was hard at work shoeing a horse when he saw the two strangers coming his way. He quit what he was doing and went to see what they wanted. "Afternoon."

"We're relatives of Rebecca Rawlins, and we need transportation out to the Circle D Ranch."

"All right. Just give me a minute to get the buggy hitched up, and we'll go." Ol' Mick was surprised the men were using Rawlins's name, but he figured since they were related to the mail-order bride, they didn't know her husband's real identity yet. He thought about telling them but decided to stay quiet, knowing they were going to find out the truth soon enough.

It wasn't long before Ol' Mick was driving the buggy around to the front of the stable to pick up the two strangers. He reined in and waited while they climbed into the buggy with him. Once they were sitting down, he slapped the reins on the horse's back, and they were on their way. He tried to make some conversation with the men at first, but they made it clear that they weren't interested in hearing anything he had to say, so he shut up.

Bryce was looking forward to the moment Destiny saw him for the first time. He couldn't wait to see the terror in her eyes when she realized he'd finally tracked her down, and she could no longer escape the consequences of what she'd done to him that night. He realized they might run into some trouble with this husband who'd sent for her, but if Rawlins became a problem, he had no doubt the man could be bought off. Every man had his price. After all, he'd bought Destiny from Raymond. Again, he thought of how she'd cheapened herself by marrying some cowboy. He was disgusted, but his revenge would be sweet, and he was ready to exact that revenge—now. Soon, very soon, the weeks of endless searching would be over, and she would be his.

The ride out to the ranch seemed to take an eternity as they covered mile after endless mile.

"How much longer will this take?" Bryce demanded in disgust.

"We're almost there," Ol' Mick assured him. "Another mile or three and we'll be able to see the ranch house. When we get there, do you want me to wait to take you back to town or go ahead and leave?"

Bryce and Raymond hadn't thought too much past just seeing Destiny again. They exchanged a quick look, trying to decide what would work best.

Raymond spoke up. "Wait for us."

"I can do that," Ol' Mick assured them before falling silent again.

Finally, the ranch house and outbuildings came into view.

"There's the main house," Ol' Mick pointed out.

Bryce and Raymond studied the layout of the buildings critically. They didn't see anyone moving around, and they weren't sure whether that was good or bad. It might mean there was no one at the ranch—including Destiny—or it might mean she was there alone, which would work out perfectly for them.

Ol' Mick drew up in front of the house and looked around, a little surprised to find there were no ranch hands in sight. "It looks kinda quiet here today. That ain't normal. I wonder if something's going on—"

"We'll go find Rebecca," Bryce said. "I'm sure she's probably in the house somewhere."

He quickly climbed down, followed by Raymond. The two men looked around, but seeing no one coming their way to greet them, they went on up to the house.

Raymond paused at the front door, wondering whether to knock or not, but Bryce didn't even give it a thought. He wanted the element of surprise on his side. He pushed open the door and walked right in.

As Destiny worked hard at what were now her normal household chores, she couldn't believe that the very next day, she and Lane would be leaving for St. Louis. For the first time since that awful night with Raymond and Bryce, she was filled with hope. Because of Lane, she no longer had to live a lie. He would stand beside her, loving her and protecting her, and she knew that with his support, she could do anything.

The last thought made her grin, because she had discovered she was turning into a decent cook, and she was learning how to keep a house. For a moment, she thought of Sylvia and realized just how hard the woman had worked for her family all those years. Sylvia definitely was a very talented, hardworking woman, as well as a wonderful friend. Destiny hoped some day she'd be able to repay Sylvia for her help escaping that night. She didn't know how she would do it, but she planned to find a way.

Destiny was in the back of the house hard at work when she heard someone come in the front door. She was surprised, wondering if it was Lane returning early. He'd told her he was riding out with Steve and the hands that morning to take one last look around before they left on their trip, so she hadn't looked for him to return until late that afternoon. She stopped what she was doing to go find him.

She was expecting to find Lane coming her way.

She was expecting to go into his arms and kiss him. She wanted to tell him how much she'd missed him during the few short hours they'd been apart.

But what she found shocked her to the depths of her being, and she froze, unable to move or speak at the sight of Raymond coming down the front hall toward her.

"Well, well, well, look what we have here . . ." Raymond said, gloating at the sight of her standing before them, looking completely stunned. He liked seeing her so disconcerted. It made him feel powerful. "Looks like we've finally found her . . ."

For a moment, Destiny was confused. She had no idea who he was talking to or what he was doing there.

And then Bryce stepped forward out of the parlor to come face-to-face with her.

"So, my dear, we meet again—at last," Bryce snarled. It pleased him to see the look of astonishment on her face. He chuckled evilly.

"Bryce . . . You're not . . ." She stared up at him, seeing the scars on his face and knowing from the savage look he was giving her just how furious he was at what she'd done to him.

"Dead?" he asked sarcastically, advancing on her.

"Oh, no, my dear, I'm quite alive and well. No thanks to you. I am a little the worse for wear, perhaps . . ." He touched his scarred face to emphasize his need for revenge. "But I'm still quite alive, my dear—and looking forward to our wedding day . . . and our wedding night." The tone he used for the last left no doubt of his intentions.

"What? You're crazy!" Destiny backed away from him as he kept coming toward her.

"Hardly, Destiny," he sneered. "I'm not crazy. I'm just a serious businessman who intends to hold you to our agreement. You were to marry me to settle your stepfather's debts. I plan to see that you abide by the agreement."

"I can't marry you!"

"Oh, but you can," he said darkly, closing in on her. "And you will."

"No! I can't! I'm already married!"

Bryce just laughed, and Raymond echoed the sound from where he was still standing in the front hall, watching all that was transpiring.

"You married a complete stranger using a fake name, and you think that marriage is valid in the eyes of the law?" Bryce challenged. "Hardly."

"Get out of my house! Both of you!"

Bryce only laughed again and closed in on her.

Chapter Twenty-four

Destiny knew she couldn't cower before Bryce. Lane had taught her to use a gun, and he'd also taught her to keep it close at hand for moments just like this. She backed toward the kitchen, knowing she'd left her gun on the small side table there.

"Get away from me!" she shouted in the hope that there might be someone close enough to hear her and realize she needed help.

Bryce and Raymond kept coming, though. They'd finally tracked her down, and they weren't about to let her get away from them again. They certainly weren't intimidated by her shouting, until . . .

Destiny reached the kitchen and quickly grabbed her gun from its holster. She spun around and aimed it straight at Bryce as he started to close in on her.

"I told you two to get away from me! Get out of my house. Leave me alone!" She glanced at her stepfather, then back to Bryce, her eyes wide with fear and loathing.

Bryce was a bit surprised that she'd pulled a gun on them, but he wasn't put off by her threat. He spoke to her condescendingly. "Destiny, what are you doing holding a gun? Put it down before you hurt yourself."

"I told you to leave me alone, and I meant it!" she declared, concentrating on keeping the revolver aimed straight at him. She was shaking, but she hoped her hand would be steady enough to get off a shot if she needed to.

Bryce was ready to wrestle the gun from her or even hit her if he had to, to knock the gun from her hand.

"You're not going to shoot me—" Bryce sneered with snide arrogance as he started to make his move on her.

Both men jumped when a deep, threatening voice sounded behind them.

"Destiny might not shoot you, but don't doubt for a minute that I will—"

Bryce and Raymond were completely startled, and they froze where they were.

"If you value your miserable lives, you'll get away from my wife," Lane ordered. "Now!"

Bryce and Raymond slowly turned around to find a tall, dangerous-looking man pointing a lethal-looking six-gun at them.

"You heard me! Move!"

The two quickly inched away from Destiny, moving back toward the man standing in the hall.

Lane had been riding homeward with Steve when he'd seen Ol' Mick driving the two strangers up to the house in the buggy. He had realized immediately from their clothing that the two men were from back East. Believing they meant trouble for Destiny, he had spurred his horse to a gallop to reach the house in time. The memory of what had happened to Katie when she'd faced Mose all alone had terrified him, and Lane wasn't about to let these two get anywhere near Destiny. When he'd hurried inside to find them threatening her, he'd known his instincts had been right.

"Now," Lane said slowly as he looked the men up and down. "Who are you, and why are you threatening my wife?"

"I am Raymond Howard, her stepfather, and this is Bryce Parker, her fiancé. We've come here to take her back home."

"Destiny is home. She's my wife, and she isn't going anywhere with you," Lane stated as he glared at them coldly, seeing what pitiful excuses they were for men.

"You know her real name?" Raymond sounded surprised.

Lane gave him an easy, yet threatening, smile as he looked from one to the other. "I know everything."

Lane was glad when he saw Bryce begin to look very uncomfortable.

Lane went on. "So I suggest you two . . . gentlemen . . . make yourselves real scarce. Get out of my house and out of my town—" He gestured toward the door with his gun. "Unless you're looking for real trouble—If you are, I'll be more than happy to oblige . . ."

Raymond was cowardly enough to hurry to the door, but Bryce looked his adversary up and down in disgust.

"You can't tell me what to do," Bryce said defiantly.

Lane knew what this man had tried to do to Destiny, and he wanted to make him pay. He moved so quickly, Bryce never saw it coming. Lane hit him as hard as he could, and then he clubbed the arrogant man on the side of his head with his six-gun and threw him bodily out the open front door. As he tossed Bryce outside, he kicked him in the seat of his pants and shoved him across the porch. Lane watched in satisfaction as Bryce tumbled down the steps and landed facedown in the dirt right in front of Steve and Ol' Mick.

"You got trouble, Boss?" Steve asked, more than ready to lend a hand.

"I don't know. Do I?" Lane looked at Raymond.

"No—No, we're leaving. Just don't hurt me," Raymond begged. "I'm going . . . I'm going . . ." He edged around Lane, terrified that he might be next to suffer his wrath.

Lane cast a quick glance toward Destiny and was

relieved to see that she looked untouched. "Are you all right?"

Tears welled up in her eyes as she put her gun down and ran to him. "I am, thanks to you . . ."

Lane kept her close by his side as they watched Raymond hurry from the porch. Lane still had his gun in hand as they moved to stand at the top of the porch steps.

"My name is Lane Madison, and I'm a Texas Ranger. Destiny is my wife, and this is my ranch. I don't take kindly to you showing up here and trying to cause trouble for me and my family," he said coldly.

Raymond had hurried to kneel down beside Bryce in the dirt. He was trying to help him up.

Bryce was furious at having been so manhandled. He indignantly shoved the older man away as he struggled to stand up. When he finally got to his feet, he spun around to face Lane. "You're not going to get away with this!"

Lane just smiled at him. "I already have."

Bryce tried to brush some of the dirt and dust off of his clothes and then looked up at Destiny where she stood beside Lane. He threatened, "This isn't over."

"Yes. It is," Lane said harshly. "If you value your miserable life, I suggest you finish dusting yourself off and get off my property right now!"

Bryce was ready to argue, but just then Ol' Mick shouted out, "Look, boys! The sheriff's riding in!"

Lane was surprised when he saw the lawman coming their way. He had no idea why Sheriff Langston would come to the Circle D, but he knew it had to be important for him to be riding that fast. Lane slowly holstered his gun as the sheriff drew up at the house.

"What's the trouble, Sheriff?" Lane asked as the lawman reined in right before them.

Sheriff Langston looked from the two strangers to Lane. "A telegram just came in for your wife. It's from a lawyer in St. Louis, and it sounds important. I thought you'd want to get it right away."

The sheriff pulled the telegram out of his pocket to hand it over, and Lane went to take it from him.

Raymond looked even more nervous as he watched Lane read the wire.

Bryce glanced at Raymond, and, seeing his stricken expression, he wondered what was going on.

"It's from your mother's lawyer, a man named Westlake," Lane told Destiny.

"What's it about?" she asked, confused.

"It says: Warning. Mr. Howard en route to Bluff Springs. Stop. Your mother's will forged. Stop. Your inheritance is waiting for you. Stop. Contact me as soon as possible."

"Oh—God . . ." Destiny began to cry as she ran to embrace Lane. She looked over at Raymond then, all the disgust she was feeling for the lying, cheating lecher plain in her eyes. "You lied about everything!

You're nothing but a thief who tried to steal all my family's money."

Bryce looked at Raymond in disbelief. "You mean you never had control of the Sterling money? Everything you told me was a lie?"

The look on Raymond's face revealed everything. He was a coward and a liar and a thief.

Unable to restrain himself, Bryce hit Raymond as hard as he could, knocking him to the ground. Bryce didn't look back but strode to the buggy and climbed in.

"Driver! Get me back to town! *Now!*" Bryce ordered.

Ol' Mick rushed to climb up into the buggy. He was grinning at all the action and excitement he'd just witnessed. He knew there was sure going to be some good gossip going around town tonight!

Raymond lay on the ground, moaning and crying and bleeding from his broken nose.

Lane went to stand over him. "Get out of here. I don't ever want to see your miserable face again! If we see or hear from you again, you're going to find the law after you for trying to steal Destiny's inheritance." Lane looked at his foreman. "Get him out of here, Steve. Have one of the boys go with him and make sure he's on the next stage out of Bluff Springs."

Steve nodded. "We'll take care of it."

Steve grabbed Raymond by the arm and jerked

him to his feet. He all but dragged the crying man away to the stable to get him on a horse so he could haul him into town.

Sheriff Langston looked at Lane and Destiny. "Are you two all right now?"

"I think we're going to be fine."

"Good. I spoke to the judge earlier, and he said we can put the ranch up for auction whenever you're ready."

Lane was thoughtful. "All right. I'll need a few days to talk to the banker in town to see if I can get the loan I'll need to buy it."

Destiny stepped forward to speak up then. She touched Lane's arm, drawing his attention. "If the telegram from my mother's lawyer is right, you won't need to borrow any more money."

Lane frowned. "What are you talking about?"

"My father's family—The Sterlings—We're rich. We'll have all the money we'll need to buy the Circle D," she told him, her eyes aglow as she gazed up at him. "You just got yourself a rich wife, Lane Madison."

Epilogue

Three Weeks Later

Reverend Moore was smiling as he looked from Lane to Destiny and concluded their wedding ceremony. "I now pronounce you man and wife. Lane, you may kiss your bride."

Lane smiled down at Destiny and then reached out to draw her to him. "I love you, Destiny Madison."

"I love you, too, Lane," she responded.

He gave her a sweet kiss, and a loud cheer went up from the crowd that had gathered at the church to celebrate this, their real wedding. They broke apart, laughing in delight as the guests came up to congratulate them.

After greeting everyone, they went to the church hall to attend the reception they'd planned. The musicians were ready to start playing as Lane led Destiny out on the dance floor for their first dance together.

He took her in his arms and began to squire her about the room.

"Destiny and Lane look so perfect together," Sylvia said to her daughter as they stood at the side of the dance floor watching the happy couple. "I still can't believe everything has turned out so well. It's been quite an adventure for Destiny, but I think it was worth it, since she ended up with Lane."

Sylvia had first met Lane just a few days before when she and Mary had arrived in Bluff Springs, and she'd known immediately that he was a fine, upstanding man.

"And it all turned out well for us, too, Mother," Mary said, smiling up at Sylvia. She was thrilled to be away from the city and the terror of her memories of that awful night when Raymond had threatened them.

"You're right. It has. I loved Destiny's mother very much, and now to be out here with Destiny and Lane—Well, life's going to be a lot better for us from now on. Thank heaven Miss Annabelle's lawyer figured out what Raymond had done. We'll never have to worry about him again," Sylvia said.

"Good." Mary paused for a moment and then couldn't help grinning.

Sylvia noticed her smile and asked, "What are you thinking about?"

Mary gave a girlish giggle as she said, "Mr. Howard sure looked silly with his broken nose."

"Yes, he did," Sylvia agreed. "And I think the look suited him just fine." She smiled at Mary. Her relief had been great when she'd learned that Raymond's deceit had been discovered, and she'd been truly honored when Destiny had sent a telegram, asking them to come to Texas live on the ranch.

Sylvia was surprised when Ol' Mick came up to them. She'd met him her first day in town, when he'd taken Mary and her out to the Circle D, and she'd thought he was a nice man.

"Miss Sylvia, would you like to dance?" Ol' Mick asked respectfully.

"Why, I'd love to." She almost felt like a young girl as she allowed him to take her out on the dance floor to join the other couples.

Mary watched her mother go and knew their lives were only going to get better now that they were in Texas.

Caroline and Steve were celebrating, too, along with the rest of the ranch hands. Now that Lane had decided to give up being a Ranger, and he and Destiny had bought the Circle D at the auction, the uncertainty they'd been living with was over. Lane had big plans for the ranch, and they were all going to work together to turn it into one of the most successful spreads in the state.

* * *

It was much later that night when Lane and Destiny returned to the ranch. It had been a long day, but a wonderful one, and they were looking forward excitedly to the night to come.

"Wait a minute, Mrs. Madison," Lane said as Destiny started to go inside ahead of him.

He took her up in his arms and carried her across the threshold, kicking the door shut behind them.

Destiny had linked her arms around his neck as she looked up at him and smiled sensuously. "Aren't you going to put me down?"

Lane didn't bother to answer her. He just kissed her instead and started straight up the steps with her still in his arms. He didn't put her down until they were in the bedroom.

"Do you want me to put on Gertrude's wedding present again?" she asked seductively.

"The only wedding present I need right now is you," he told her.

And Destiny gave him the best gift of all.

She gave him her love.

☐ **YES!**

Sign me up for the Historical Romance Book Club and send my FREE BOOKS! If I choose to stay in the club, I will pay only $8.50* each month, a savings of $6.48!

NAME: _____

ADDRESS: _____

TELEPHONE: _____

EMAIL: _____

☐ I want to pay by credit card.

☐ **VISA** ☐ **MasterCard** ☐ **DISCOVER**

ACCOUNT #: _____

EXPIRATION DATE: _____

SIGNATURE: _____

Mail this page along with $2.00 shipping and handling to:
Historical Romance Book Club
PO Box 6640
Wayne, PA 19087
Or fax (must include credit card information) to:
610-995-9274

You can also sign up online at **www.dorchesterpub.com**.
*Plus $2.00 for shipping. Offer open to residents of the U.S. and Canada only. Canadian residents please call 1-800-481-9191 for pricing information.
If under 18, a parent or guardian must sign. Terms, prices and conditions subject to change. Subscription subject to acceptance. Dorchester Publishing reserves the right to reject any order or cancel any subscription.